Where had Alice _____ *ht stealing was the* _____ *s? "Burl, stealing wa* _____

She mustered her courage and turned back to Mr. MacGregor. She hoped he would be understanding. "Are you going to notify the police?"

"Not if a couple of conditions are met."

"I'll pay for the window." When she got a job.

"That won't be necessary. Burl will come to work for me before school and after school until it's paid off."

He wasn't going to notify the police. She gave a sigh of relief. He was a nice man. "That's very generous of you."

"I can go with him to make sure he does as he is told," Grandpa said.

"That won't be necessary, Mr. Greig. Burl will do as he's told. Won't you, boy?"

"Yes, sir."

"I do have one other condition. You come to work for me, too."

She jerked her gaze to his face. "What?"

"I could use another assistant at the store."

He was going to use her poor circumstance against her. "I'm afraid that won't be possible."

"Did you secure other employment?"

"No, but. . ." She didn't want him using this to take advantage of the situation. She wanted him to stay a nice man.

"Then you'll come work for me. I insist."

She looked from him to Burl to Grandpa. Tears welled, and she strode to her room. Latching the door, she leaned against it. *Dear Lord, what do I do? Is Mr. MacGregor using my poor circumstances and Burl's bad behavior to take advantage? Please let him just be a nice man with no ulterior motives.*

An alliance with Mr. MacGregor was tenuous at best. She was afraid. Afraid of him. Afraid of what he might do. . .to her heart. She couldn't trust herself where men were concerned. She had poor judgment. Very poor judgment.

MARY DAVIS is a full-time writer whose first published novel was *Newlywed Games*. She enjoys going into schools and talking to kids about writing. Mary lives near Colorado's Rocky Mountains with her husband, three teens, and seven pets. Please visit her Web site at http://marydavisbooks.com.

Books by Mary Davis

HEARTSONG PRESENTS
HP399—Cinda's Surprise
HP436—Marty's Ride
HP514—Roger's Return
HP653—Lakeside
HP669—The Island
HP682—The Grand Hotel
HP690—Heritage

Uncertain
Alliance

Mary Davis

Heartsong Presents

Dedicated to my children, Ben, Josh, and Jessi. And to the men and women over the decades who have made the underground Seattle what it is. And to Bill Speidel for bringing the underground back to life.

A note from the Author:
I love to hear from my readers! You may correspond with me by writing:

Mary Davis
Author Relations
PO Box 721
Uhrichsville, OH 44683

ISBN 978-1-59789-901-7

UNCERTAIN ALLIANCE

Our mission is to publish and distribute inspirational products offering exceptional value and biblical encouragement to the masses.

PRINTED IN THE U.S.A.

one

Seattle, January 1895

"Straight to school. Do you hear me?" Alice Dempsey planted her hands on her slim hips and narrowed her eyes at her eleven-year-old brother, Burl.

"Why do I gotta go anyway? Mr. Kray don't know nothin'." Burl's shaggy blond hair stuck out in odd places.

"Mr. Kray *doesn't* know *anything*. And you obviously don't know everything."

"I already know everything he knows. He ain't worth shucks. He's an ignorant ol' coot." Burl jammed his hands into the pockets of his patched pants.

"That's enough of that kind of talk. He was smart enough to stick with his schooling." She tried to smooth down his cowlick with her hand.

He ducked out of her reach. "Why can't I just stay home with Grandpa?"

"Schooling is important." She didn't want Burl to end up spending the rest of his life in a dirty, overpriced, overcrowded apartment. He deserved a place to run and play. She turned to their grandfather, who sat at the rickety square table. "Talk to him."

Grandpa turned his sternest look on Burl. "Do as your sister says. I wish I would've had an opportunity to go to school."

Burl got a twinkle in his blue eyes. "You go in my place. Tell Mr. Kray you're me. He'd probably believe it, too. He's that stupid."

Grandpa narrowed his green eyes. "Put on your shoes and skedaddle, young man." Then he coughed several times, hard.

5

She worried over Grandpa. The medicine she'd spent the last of her money on didn't seem to be helping so far. And his heart wasn't very strong. She needed him. He was her rock, her anchor.

Burl gave in but muttered through the whole process about its being a waste of time. When he stood, three-year-old Miles held his hands up to him. Burl picked him up. "Hey, squirt, your time's a comin'. Your mean ole ma's gonna make you go to school, too."

Alice took Miles, setting him on her hip, and handed Burl his lunch pail with only a boiled potato and a bread crust to satisfy his hunger. He was too thin. "Straight to school."

He let out a long burp.

"Burl, mind your manners."

He nodded then grinned, heading for the apartment door.

She watched him walk down the hall. He was growing so tall, almost as tall as her at five foot five inches. His voice had begun to crack when he spoke. The first of many steps to becoming a man.

When he turned to go down the stairs, she could see his mouth flapping open and closed, but no words were coming out. Still a boy. She wished he wouldn't mock her when he thought she wasn't looking, but as long as he went to school, she'd overlook it. She understood his desire to contribute to the family. She was providing fine for them right now. The day would come soon enough when he would need to work as well, but for now, she wanted him to get as much schooling as possible. At least finish this school year.

She shut the door and turned to Grandpa. "Thanks for helping with Burl."

"He's right, you know."

"Please don't start." She set Miles in a chair to eat his oatmeal.

"He *is* smarter than Mr. Kray. But you're right, too. He should be in school as long as he can. He needs a strong hand.

I wish I were more help to you instead of one more burden." Grandpa held up his stump arm that ended just below his elbow.

She knelt beside Grandpa's chair. "You are not a burden."

He touched her cheek. "I wish you had someone to take care of you."

"The four of us are doing just fine." She hadn't done so well choosing a husband for herself though. "Will you be fine with Miles?"

"You ask me that every day. I near on raised your ma by myself. I daresay we'll manage." Grandpa patted her hand.

"I worry about you."

"I know you do. I worry about you, too."

"You look so tired all the time." Maybe she should let Burl stay home and help Grandpa.

Grandpa tapped his chest. "This old body don't sleep like it used to."

"It doesn't help that you can't nap during the day." She glanced at her very active three-year-old son.

"I'd sleep better at night if you had someone to look after you." His green gaze bore into her.

"I don't want you wearing yourself out worrying over me. I need you. I can't do all this by myself." She glanced around their meager two-room flat.

"I know. That's why I worry and why you need a husband." Grandpa unfolded the newspaper on the table in front of him.

"Grandpa, don't even suggest it. Oscar turned out to be my worst decision ever. Nothing good came of it." She ruffled Miles's wad of curly blond hair. "Except for him, of course." Looking back, she could tell that she'd been sad and still mourning the loss of her ma two months earlier. Oscar had probably sensed her vulnerability.

"Just be picking more carefully this time."

There wasn't going to be a *this time* or a next time. She swung on her shawl then kissed Grandpa on the cheek. "Don't overdo it today." She shook her finger at him.

"Don't be pointing at me, young lady."

She tucked her finger away and straightened her back. Young lady indeed. She wasn't even twenty-two and already felt eighty. She kissed Miles on the head. "You be good for Grandpa."

Miles smiled up at her. "I be dood."

"I don't know why they bother printing the tide schedule anymore." Grandpa had turned to his newspaper. "With the streets raised, people can flush their toilet anytime they like." Poor Grandpa. He was left to reading newspapers that were several days old. But he never complained. He liked to read it as though it was today's. He'd learned to read as an adult when her ma had learned. In the evenings, he'd ask her everything she learned in school. He'd take it all in without letting on to his young daughter that he was learning from her.

"People like to know the tide schedule for more than just plumbing utility." There had been plans to raise the city streets to correct the plumbing issues that rose with the tide twice daily, but six years ago, a poor Swedish cabinet employee inadvertently started a fire that burned thirty city blocks. He became a hero. The ugly haphazard town had a chance to rebuild itself into a cleaner, more refined city. The plans to raise the streets were all the talk, but the business owners didn't trust the city planners to get the job completed quickly; they rebuilt their businesses of brick and stone, knowing the streets would be raised around them in the near future.

"Look at this." He pointed to the open page. "Another poor drunk fell off the street. Fortunately, it was one with a short drop. Broke both ankles, his arm, his collarbone, and gave himself a concussion."

The city had been slow in raising the streets and even slower in constructing the sidewalks from the street to the front of the buildings. Not all the sidewalks were finished. "Serves him right for taking the devil's drink."

"Now, Alice, that's not very charitable."

"Oscar drank, gambled, and the Lord only knows what else with what little money we had. Left us with nothing. I have no tolerance for a man who drinks." The mention of Oscar caused all sorts of feelings to rise in her; anger and hurt at his lies and deception, longing for what she thought they'd had, and regret for Miles's not having a good father to help raise him to become an upstanding man.

Grandpa turned back to his paper.

"I need to skedaddle, too, or I'll be late." She took one last pensive look at Grandpa and headed out the door. She crossed the muddy street and headed for the schoolhouse. Burl was skipping rocks on an oversized puddle in the schoolyard. One worry down. She headed up the street and toward downtown. Cold water and mud seeped through the crack in the side of her boot, soaking her stocking. At least the rain from last night had stopped, or she'd be soaked from head to toe.

She walked up the incline of the first paved street of her trek and tried to shake off as much mud from her boots as possible. Then she came to the first raised street. She looked to the sidewalk fifteen feet below. It would be faster to stay up above, but she didn't want to have the same fate as the man in the paper. Even sober people could fall to their demise. She went to the corner and climbed down the hastily constructed wooden stairs to the boardwalk below. The stairs had been built as a temporary measure to get up and down from the street. Above her, five-foot-wide bridges connected the street to the second-floor doorways. She walked the block and greeted a couple of store owners who were just beginning to open up. Half of the first floors on the edge of the reconstruction didn't have any businesses in them but were used for storage. Others housed businesses of ill repute and were open under the cover of darkness. Many claimed to have an abundance of seamstresses, but word had it that not so much as a single threaded needle could be found on their premises. She needed to hurry along so she wouldn't be late. She didn't want to give her boss any excuse to fire her. She was already on slippery mud with the woman.

Up one rickety staircase and down another and up again. If the sidewalks weren't completed soon, the staircases would need to be replaced. Once above ground again, she could cross the street and round one of the blocks that had overhead sidewalks. It was a wonder that they had raised the streets around the buildings and were now constructing sidewalks from the street to the buildings. She descended sturdy paved stairs on a side street and through a doorway to the sidewalk below. As she approached the corner, she looked up at the checkered glass skylight in the sidewalk above. Even on a cloudy day, the skylights poured light onto the walkways below. When she rounded the corner, she wanted to turn back. Ian MacGregor was washing the front windows of his pharmacy next door to the millinery where she worked. She would be late if she waited until he was finished.

She used to come early to be able to talk with him for a few minutes. He was kind and always had a gentle word. As of late she'd sensed that maybe his friendship toward her was becoming something more. The last thing she wanted to do was encourage feelings on his side. He stood on a ladder to reach the tops of the windows. She dipped her head and continued past the bookshop, the hair salon, shoe repair store, and pharmacy to the millinery, hoping he would be too busy to take notice of her.

As she passed by, he turned. "Good day, Miss Dempsey."

It was missus, but she'd never bothered to correct him. Also, she liked to ignore that one bit of poor judgment in her life. "Good day, Mr. MacGregor."

"You are looking well today." He gazed at her with a look that said more than his words.

She caught the hint of his Scottish brogue. She wanted

to ask him about it but didn't want to be so forward. "As are you." She ducked into the millinery before a part of her decided to bask in his kindness and warm brown eyes.

❧

Ian MacGregor stared at Tilly's Millinery shop door. Alice had slipped away. Again. He'd hoped she'd get to work early so they could talk as they once had, but of late she'd been getting to work just in time for opening.

The bell over his own shop's door jingled, and Conner Jackson stepped out.

Ian had hired Conner the day he'd rented his underground store space. Conner had been inquiring about employment from Mr. Lansky upstairs, who owned the building. Ian had felt a connection to Conner from the first moment and had prayed on the spot, and the Lord had led him to offer the younger man a job. By the end of that week, Conner had moved his few belongings into the back of the pharmacy, appreciative of a place to stay. Conner had quickly become his best friend in the new city Ian was calling home. The Lord had given Ian a fresh start.

Conner looked toward the millinery. "Did you get to talk to her?"

He climbed down off the ladder. "Who?"

"Who indeed?" Conner took the bucket of water. "I doubt the windows have gotten dirty since you washed them yesterday. If you aren't washing the windows, you're sweeping the boardwalk or checking your sign or whatever it is you do when you're standing out here doing nothing, looking at the storefront."

"Am I that obvious?" He folded the ladder.

Conner held the door and followed him inside. "To me you are. I don't think Miss Dempsey has noticed."

"She's not likely to notice the likes of me." He put the ladder in the storage room.

Conner dumped the nearly clean water down the drain.

"Why do you say that?"

"Look at me, Conner. I'm not a handsome dude like you. I'm barely five foot and six inches. Ladies prefer men like you who are tall and lean. And certainly a young lady as beautiful as Alice would want a man who is more than an inch taller than her." He looked up at Conner. His pent-up frustration came out in a deep breath. "When I'm standing next to you, no lady would even notice I was there." He ran a hand over his thinning sandy hair. It had nothing distinguishing about it. It was about as appealing as the mud puddles after the rain. Not at all like Alice's. Hers was a beautiful pale blond, almost white like an angel's. And he suspected it was wavy, too, by the looks of the curly tendrils around her face.

"You have a lot to offer a lady." Conner gripped his shoulder. "Once she gets to know you, she'll see that."

He'd like to believe that. "I've learned that beautiful women have only one interest when it comes to me."

"What's that?" Conner put the bucket under the sink and pulled out a box of rags.

He patted his breast pocket. "My wallet."

"You aren't giving Miss Dempsey much credit. She seems like a hardworking young lady. The kind who makes her own way in this world."

"So it seems."

Conner dug in the rags and pulled out the metal cash box. He handed it to Ian. "If Miss Dempsey was after money, why would she be working at a shop underground?"

He couldn't answer that. "She's playing on my sympathies?"

"The way you talk, she can't even see you." Conner cocked one eyebrow. "If you're so determined to think she's after money, why stay sweet on her?"

"I don't think she is after money yet. But if she were to turn her attention toward me, what other reason could it be but money?"

Conner shook his head. "You are hopeless. Who put you in

such a foul mood on ladies?"

Ian headed for the front of the store and opened the cash register. "Before I came out here a year ago and opened shop, I was engaged to a beautiful woman." He made sure he was looking away from Conner when he made this confession. He didn't want to see the shocked look on Conner's face.

"Obviously she only wanted money." Conner didn't sound shocked, so he looked back at him.

"It wasn't just the money; it was what she wanted it for."

Conner waggled his head back and forth. "I can't even imagine."

He slowly counted the money into the drawer. "Charity."

Conner hesitated before he spoke. "Why was that a problem?"

He straightened the bills and coins. "There was a certain wealthy gentleman, who was handsome to boot, intimately involved with this charity. She wanted him to take notice of her. She used my money to gain his attention."

"Ouch."

"They are happily married now and, as I hear it, expecting their first child." He closed the drawer harder than need be.

Conner was silent for a moment. "I don't think Miss Dempsey is like that. If she were after money, she'd be up there." He pointed up toward the street level. "She would have no trouble finding half a dozen men to buy her fine things."

"I didn't think Azalea was like that either, obviously."

"So what's Miss Dempsey's story?"

He went to the door and rolled up the shade, signifying they were open. "I haven't been bold enough to ask her. I don't want her to think I'm prying."

Conner leaned on the shelf behind the counter and folded his arms. "So you have no idea if her parents would even approve of you courting their daughter?"

"I have no idea if she even lives with her parents. She

seems so independent and never mentioned them. For all I know, she has a beau or husband." He hoped not.

"No men come by the millinery calling on her, and there doesn't seem to be a man buying her expensive clothes. So what have you spoken to her about?"

"I tell her she is looking well. One of us will mention the weather, the other how the construction on the streets and boardwalk is progressing. She's very intelligent."

Conner pushed off the shelf. "That's it? In all these weeks of standing out front making yourself busy?"

"Oh no. We've conversed on the feud between the Dennys and the other founding fathers. And on Doc Maynard."

Conner stared at him like he'd just told him he was going to invite a grizzly bear home for dinner. "Have either of you ever spoken about yourselves?"

He shook his head. "I'm not bold with ladies as you are. I don't know what to say."

"I wouldn't say I'm bold around ladies, but I can talk to them. Miss Dempsey is a person. Just talk to her like you do me."

He widened his eyes. "I could never do that."

"Yes, you can. Just use a little restraint." Conner put his hand on Ian's shoulder. "This is what you're going to do: Just before closing time, you are going to go over to Tilly's Millinery and ask Miss Dempsey if you can walk her home."

At the thought, Ian's lungs seemed to stop. "What if she turns me down?"

"Then you will ask her again tomorrow and the next day and the next until she weakens and says yes. Then you will tell her about yourself, where you grew up, and how you became interested in pharmaceuticals. Then she will likely tell you about herself."

"You make it sound so easy."

"It is. How did you meet Azalea and what did the two of you talk about?"

"We bumped into each other on the street. Her parcels fell

to the ground. I helped her with them and walked her home. She did most of the talking."

Conner thinned his lips and shook his head. "A vixen. She manipulated you from the start."

"You think so?" He didn't want to think badly of Azalea, so he tried not to think of her at all and succeeded most of the time.

"I've seen it before. It was no accident that you ran into her that day. But Miss Dempsey is no vixen."

"Just because Miss Dempsey isn't—as you put it—a vixen, doesn't mean she will ever hold any affection for me. She's more likely to be interested in you."

"If I am such a detriment to your romantic endeavors"— Conner folded his arms—"why did you hire me and let me move into one of the back rooms?"

"You needed a job, and I found you trustworthy from the start." He folded his arms as well, but it didn't have the same daunting effect as it did on Conner. "If you find Miss Dempsey so attractive, why haven't you asked to walk her home?"

Conner squared his broad shoulders. "First of all, you're sweet on her. I wouldn't cross that line even for a lady I was loopy for. I'd clear out before I'd try to take a friend's sweetheart. No woman is worth the cost of a good friend."

"Alice isn't my sweetheart." Not that he didn't wish it so.

"Close enough for me. Second reason is I'm not interested in Miss Dempsey or love right now. I want to start my own business. I want to have a way to provide for a wife and family first."

It was easy enough to think you had control of love, another altogether to actually control it and choose with whom and when to fall in love. "I was determined never to fall for a lady again. What if love sneaks up on you as it has me?"

Conner considered that a moment then smiled. "I guess I'll have to kick myself in the head."

That was not a solution he'd want to try.

The bell over the door jingled, announcing the arrival of a customer and ending their conversation, but Ian could definitely ask to walk Alice home. Her answer would tell him a lot.

two

Alice glanced at the clock over the door as her fingers nimbly worked the needle in and out of Mrs. Brown's new velvet hat. She should have it completed just in time for closing. Mrs. Brown would be in early tomorrow to either approve it or request changes.

She stood and stretched her back. Miss Tilly, a fleshy woman in her fifties, stepped through the curtain into the workroom and glared at her. She quickly sat back down, but before she could pick up her needle, Miss Tilly said, "Don't bother sittin'. You're wanted out front."

She stood. "Me?"

Miss Tilly frowned. "Be quick about it. That hat needs to be finished today."

She ducked through the curtain and saw a police officer. *Oh no. Burl.* What else could it be? Not something wrong with Grandpa.

She walked up to the officer. "I'm Alice Dempsey."

He turned his hat in his hands. "Officer Blake, ma'am. Do you know a Burl Martin?"

Her heart sank. "He's my brother."

"He's been cutting didoes down at the docks. I'll need you to come with me."

Mischief, mischief, mischief. Must he always land himself in a lick of trouble? She sighed and hurried to the back to get her handbag and shawl.

"You leaving?" Miss Tilly said with her hands on her hips.

"It's my brother. I have to." She swung on her shawl.

"What about Mrs. Brown's hat?"

"I'll come in early and finish."

Miss Tilly just shook her head.

Alice snatched up her handbag and hurried back out to the officer.

❧

Ian escorted stoop-shouldered Mr. Piedmont to the door and held it for him while he shuffled out. It was amazing that Mr. Piedmont could even make it down to the lower-level shops. Ian appreciated a faithful customer but wondered if a street-level business would be more beneficial.

The light was fading from the overhead skylights. Clouds were building. By the intensity of the light, he could just about always tell what the weather was up above. He'd better grab his umbrella before he offered to walk Miss Dempsey home. He didn't want her getting wet.

As though the thought of her had conjured her up, Miss Dempsey came out of the millinery—followed by an officer of the law. "Alice? I mean Miss Dempsey."

She glanced his way then hurried off. Where was she going? He wanted to follow, but Conner wouldn't return for another half hour and he still had a customer inside. *Lord, please be with Alice in whatever trouble she is going to find.*

❧

Alice pulled her shawl tighter and tried not to breathe too deeply. The pungent smell of dead fish and rotting debris polluted her lungs. The wind coming off the sound was chillier than in town and helped to cleanse the air a little. She climbed the plank up onto the ship to a floor that rocked beneath her. Burl sprang to his feet when he saw her approach, but the sailor next to him put a hand to Burl's shoulder, pressing him back down onto the barrel.

She hurried over to Burl. "What have you done?"

Burl looked down at his worn brogans with a hole in one toe. "Nothin'."

"He and his two buddies threw a couple of lard barrels overboard. Wanted to see if they would float."

She spun to the sound of the surly voice behind her. The captain stood tall and lean in his neatly pressed uniform. A handsome cut of a man if it weren't for his intimidating scowl. She wanted to cower like a lost kitten.

"This is Captain Carlyle, captain of this vessel," Officer Blake said.

The captain stood broad shouldered, towering over her. Thick brown whiskers covered the lower half of his face and matched his wavy brown mane. He narrowed his gray eyes, intending to intimidate her, she was sure. It was working.

"I'll pay for any damages my brother has caused." Her voice barely squeaked out, making her sound like a lost kitten.

The captain glowered at her then at Burl. He seemed to be waiting.

"I don't have any money with me, but—"

"Then what good is your promise? I prefer to work the debt out of the boy. He's the one who caused the trouble."

Her insides clenched at the thought of losing Burl to a life at sea. "He's just a child."

Captain Carlyle's hair stirred in the breeze. "He's big enough for a cabin boy."

Burl sail away on a ship? She'd never see him again. "What about the other two boys you mentioned? Maybe their parents will pay you the damage and I can pay them back."

"Ran off faster than greased lightning. Shoved this one behind to get away." He inclined his head toward Burl. "He stays on my ship until he has worked off the debt. I sail at the next high tide."

By the tide schedule Grandpa had read this morning and adjusting for the few days later it was, today's high tide should be early this evening. "You can't keep him on this ship and sail with him."

"I can and I will." He narrowed his eyes and leaned closer to her. "Unless you want to be sailing with us as well, I suggest you make your way back to land." The captain tossed his gaze to the sailor beside Burl. "Keep a strong hand on that one until we are well out to sea." He turned and walked away.

Burl's blue eyes were wide and his face paler than his hair. "Alice, don't let them take me!"

What could she do? Maybe Miss Tilly would give her an advance on her pay. Could she go and get back in time? She went to the bottom of the stairs where Captain Carlyle had ascended to a smaller upper deck. "Captain, I'm going to go get money. Please don't sail until I return."

The captain didn't acknowledge her in any way but continued to talk to a sailor with large, tattooed muscles.

"Captain? Captain?" She could not allow him to ignore her. She climbed the stairs and approached from behind him. The sailor facing the captain glanced at her. He widened his eyes and shook his head.

She took a deep breath. "Captain."

The captain stopped talking then flipped his hand toward the sailor. The sailor gave a small nod and retreated to the other side of the small deck.

"I'm going to get money. Please don't sail before I return."

The captain turned slowly to her. His cold gray gaze pierced her. "The tide waits for no man."

She swallowed hard. "Tell me how much, and I'll return swiftly."

He studied her a moment. "Is your brother as tenacious as you are?"

She wasn't quite sure what he was getting at. "What do you mean?"

He leaned a little closer and spoke softly. "Will he try to run away?"

She hoped so. But she wasn't about to tell the captain that.

"What did you say your name was, miss?"

"Dempsey. Alice Dempsey."

"Miss Dempsey, I no more want to see you back here than

I want to have that troublesome little rat of a boy on my ship. He would only get in the way and probably cry for mama. My men would likely throw him overboard for the sharks before we reach the horizon."

She gasped. "Then why take him with you?"

"I'm not." The captain gave her a genuine smile that reached clear to his eyes as he winked at her.

"But you said—"

"I said what I said to scare the boy. Maybe this will teach him never to let older boys rope him into doing something like this again. At the very least, he'll never step foot on my ship again."

She held her breath, daring to hope. "So you are going to let him go?"

"No."

Her heart sank. "But. . ."

"We are going to keep a close eye on him just until we sail." The captain glanced toward Burl. "As we make preparation to get under way, he'll be left unguarded. So, my earlier question still stands: Will he run away?"

"I think so."

"Good. Now I'm going to raise my voice to you; then I'm going to order my first mate to remove you from my ship. Forcibly of course."

Captain Carlyle wasn't the scoundrel she first thought he was. "You will let Burl go?"

"He has only to run away when given the opportunity."

"What if he doesn't?"

"I'll have one of my men *help* him escape."

"Thank you, Captain Carlyle. I won't forget your kindness."

He nodded. "Remember not to go quietly." He scowled then and raised his voice to a booming volume. "I said the boy stays!"

Even though she knew he was only playacting, he was still scary. She put her hands on her hips. "I'm not leaving without my brother." Her voice shook and was not nearly as convincing as the captain's.

"Isaac, see that this wench finds her way off my ship," the captain ordered.

She quickly scooted down the stairs and headed for Burl but was grabbed from behind.

"Cap'n said you was to leave. . .off the reel." Isaac turned her toward the boarding plank, almost shoving her against another man.

"Miss Dempsey." A lanky man with brown hair reached out for her. His attire suggested a landlubber like herself rather than a seaman.

He looked familiar. "Do I know you?"

"Conner Jackson. I work for Ian MacGregor next to the millinery."

She could place him now. She'd seen him inside the pharmacy when she spoke with Mr. MacGregor on the boardwalk.

Mr. Jackson scowled at the sailor who had a grip on her arm. "Release her."

"Cap'n said to *escort* the lady off the ship."

Mr. Jackson looked up toward the captain. "Randolph, what's going on here?"

"Mr. Jackson," she whispered, "please, it's all right."

Mr. Jackson looked from her to Captain Carlyle, who was suddenly with them. "Randolph, what's the meaning of this?"

"Isaac is seeing to it that Miss Dempsey makes it safely off my ship."

"Alice!"

The foursome turned toward Burl.

"Don't leave me here!"

Mr. Jackson turned back to the captain. "And the boy?"

The captain lowered his voice. "Just putting a bit of a scare into him. He thinks I'm going to sail with him aboard."

"Captain Carlyle promised to let him escape before they set sail," she whispered.

Mr. Jackson frowned and spoke softly but sternly. "Randolph, the boy looks plenty scared now, and must you have Miss Dempsey manhandled?"

"Well, she wasn't willing to leave her brother behind."

Mr. Jackson's gaze darted from her to Burl and back again. "I think you've made your point. Let them both go."

Captain Carlyle nodded to Isaac, who took his beefy hand off her arm.

She thanked the captain and Mr. Jackson then ran to Burl. The sailor released him. She took Burl and hurried down the plank back onto solid land. She wanted to get as far from the docks as quickly as possible before the captain changed his mind. She was glad Mr. Jackson had come along so she didn't have to wait around until high tide for Burl to escape.

❧

Ian looked over his glasses as Conner strode through the door of the pharmacy. "Sorry I'm late. There was trouble down on the docks." Conner had been running an errand for him and usually stopped by the dock when his friend the captain was in port.

"It doesn't matter. Miss Dempsey left work early with a police officer. I wish I knew what that was all about. I hope she's not in trouble."

"Well, let's close up, and I'll tell you all about it."

Conner knew something? Ian quickly locked the door and pulled the shade down. "How do you know about Miss Dempsey?"

"She was involved with the trouble on the docks."

"I can't believe that." Miss Dempsey would never do anything to warrant trouble.

"It seems she has a mischievous younger brother whom she's responsible for." Conner conveyed the whole story as he'd heard it from his friend the ship's captain.

He threw up his hands. "Well, that fixes my flint."

"What does?"

"You and Miss Dempsey. I reckon she'll be setting her cap for you now."

"If you're insinuating that I'm going to take up with Miss Dempsey, you're mistaken. She doesn't even know me."

"But you rescued her from the evil pirate captain." He hated to think of her on a ship with a bunch of rough sailors. She was so delicate and beautiful. There was probably more than one of the sailors who fancied ideas of her, maybe even the captain himself.

"Randolph is no pirate."

"But you said he was surly and having her physically thrown off his ship; she'll likely view him as kindly as she would a pirate. With one look, she would probably swoon into your arms."

Conner shook his head. "Don't hang up your fiddle. I am not going to try to court Miss Dempsey. I told you she holds no interest for me."

"If not you, then it will be some other handsome bloke." He opened the cash register and began counting the money.

"You are really death on Miss Dempsey, aren't you?"

He ran a hand over his thinning hair. "Since the first time I spoke to her, God put her into my heart."

Conner eyed him from the other side of the counter. "You really believe God put her in your heart?"

He nodded. "I was never so happy that Azalea ran off with another man as the day I met Miss Dempsey."

"Let me make sure we are talking about the same God. God who made the heavens and the earth. God who made all the plants and animals. God who made all of mankind. That God, right?"

He nodded again. The main reason he got on so well with Conner from the start and trusted him almost immediately was their common faith.

"God's pretty powerful. More powerful than man?"

"Of course. Do you have a point, Conner?"

"If the God of the universe put Miss Dempsey in your heart, how could a mere mortal like me steal her away? Who can change the plans of God?"

"I never thought of it that way."

"So do you believe God put her in your heart?"

He thought he did but hesitated. "Yes."

Conner smiled. "I promise to be here tomorrow so you can walk Miss Dempsey home."

Once again Conner had proven himself a true friend. Ian would be sorry when the day came that Conner moved on.

three

Ian caught a glimpse of Miss Dempsey as she hurried by his pharmacy window earlier than usual. His pulse quickened. He went to the door, hoping to catch her and talk with her before she entered the millinery. He stepped outside but stopped when he saw her boss talking to her outside the shop.

Miss Tilly Morgan's fists were planted firmly on her fleshy hips. "Irma had to stay late to finish your work. This is the fifth time you've left work undone."

"I'm sorry. It was an urgent family matter."

"I'm sorry, too." Miss Morgan's voice was even, yet firm. "You are a very good seamstress, but I have to let you go. I have no other choice. I have a business to run."

"But I need this job." Alice's eyes widened, and he could see fear in their blue depths.

"I need someone I can depend on."

"You can depend on me."

"That's what you promised last time." Miss Morgan held out her hand. "Here is your pay minus what I had to pay Irma for finishing your work."

"I promise it won't happen again."

Ian's heart ached as Alice begged for her job.

"I'm sorry." Miss Morgan turned up Alice's hand and placed the money in it, then walked inside her shop.

Miss Dempsey stared at the shop door then turned to leave but stopped short when she saw him.

He took a step forward. "I'm so sorry."

She just stared at him with tears gathering in her eyes.

He held out a hand to her. "Please come inside."

She shook her head, and a single tear trickled down her cheek. Then she put her feet in motion and strode past him.

He wanted to reach out to her but instead said, "Please, Miss Dempsey. I'll give you the money."

She quickened her step and scurried around the corner like a frightened mouse.

He went back inside his store, shaking his head. "That was about the stupidest thing you could have said." He kicked the edge of the counter.

"Hey, my boss won't like it too well if you go tearing up his shop." Conner came from the back room with his brown hair tousled and still damp, but he was dressed in a three-piece suit. "What has your bat's-wing in a wad?"

He pulled at the thin bowtie at his neck. "Miss Morgan just let Miss Dempsey go because she had to leave work yesterday over that whole business down at the docks."

"That's not your fault."

"What I said is." He rubbed his face. "Now she probably thinks I'm a gutter rat."

"It can't be all that bad."

"I offered her money. There is only one possible conclusion why an older man, at lest ten years her senior, would offer money to a beautiful young lady in need."

"Is that what you were offering?"

He jerked his gaze to Conner. "Of course not!"

Conner raised one eyebrow. "Then apparently there are at least two possible conclusions."

"But which will she come to? I have no way of finding her to let her know my real intent. She won't be coming back to work next door, and I don't know where she lives." He sighed. "She's lost to me." An ache rose in him as if his heart were crying.

Conner clasped him on the shoulder with one hand and slapped his chest with the other. "God put her in your heart. He'll bring her back. I'll pray He brings her through your door."

Yes, prayer. He would get down on his knees and pray for her. Pray the Lord would comfort her in her time of trouble and provide her with a new job. A job that was close by so he might see her again.

~

Alice spent the rest of the day inquiring about jobs and confirmed that bad news indeed traveled faster than greased lightning. Several business owners had heard about her brother's troublesome behavior and declined to employ her. They didn't want her brother vandalizing their property. She really couldn't blame them. She didn't know what Burl would do next. He seemed to be cutting more and more didoes. Maybe she should leave him home with Grandpa. She just feared it would be too much on Grandpa's weak heart.

When she stepped inside her apartment, relief washed over her to see Burl seated at the table and not out causing trouble. He and Miles were playing a stacking tower disk game her Grandpa had whittled for her ma before he lost his arm. Burl was explaining how to move the disks one at a time from one of the three towers to the other, never putting a larger disk on top of a smaller one. The game became more difficult the more disks that were used. Burl was showing Miles with just three disks. By the time Burl was five, he had mastered all eight disks.

Grandpa lay sleeping on the straw mattress he shared with Burl in the corner.

Miles turned to her. "Ma!" he yelled and ran to her.

She scooped him up into her arms. "Shh. Grandpa's sleeping."

"I'm awake. I was just resting my eyes." Grandpa rolled to a sitting position and pulled out his pocket watch. "You're home early."

"I'm tired. I spent all day searching for a job."

"What happened with Miss Morgan?" Grandpa struggled, trying to get to his feet.

She went and put an arm around him to help. "She let me go because I left early yesterday to keep Burl from sailing with a bunch of surly seamen."

Burl dipped his head, trying to appear contrite. . .and succeeding. But she wouldn't let his sorrowful look quench her anger. They had very little money or food. And with no one willing to give her a job, she didn't know what they were going to do.

Grandpa stood with his hands clasped behind his back next to Burl. "What do you have to say for yourself, son?"

"I'm sorry, Alice. I didn't mean no harm. We was just cuttin' shines."

"Your fun has cost Alice her job. Your sister works very hard to put food on the table for all of us." Grandpa struggled not to cough.

She knew he was suffering. She was hoping to have enough money to get him medicine, but now. . . *Lord, protect his health.*

Grandpa pointed toward the stove. "You fix supper tonight."

Burl's eyes enlarged, and he stared at Grandpa. "Cookin's woman's work."

"Tonight it's your work."

"But I don't know how." Burl stood and held out his hands.

"If you're too smart for school, then you're smart enough to figure it out."

Burl could tell Grandpa was serious. Grandpa had evidently had enough of Burl's shenanigans, as well. Burl shuffled toward the stove.

Grandpa held out a chair for her. "Sit."

She did, setting Miles on her lap. "I should go help him."

"You'll do no such thing. Woman's work indeed. I did all the cookin' for your ma and me until she was old enough to do it."

"But he—"

"He'll make do. You shouldn't have to do everything. I'll go tell him how to start, and he can figure out the rest."

Grandpa bent over in a coughing fit.

She stood. "Let me."

"Sit. I'm fine." Grandpa took a few labored breaths and headed for the stove.

They had enough for supper tonight, but what about tomorrow? The money Miss Tilly had paid her would need to be given off the reel to Mr. Henderson for rent. He wouldn't wait any longer. She heard Grandpa directing Burl. "Only use one potato and one carrot," she called. With the can of beans, that should be enough. It would have to be. That left only two potatoes and a carrot for supper tomorrow night. The last of the oatmeal would be eaten for breakfast, but that would give her another day to find work and buy food.

Lord, find me work tomorrow. Don't let my family go hungry. You said in the Bible You would take care of Your own. "I have been young, and now am old; yet have I not seen the righteous forsaken, nor his seed begging bread." The verse from the book of Psalms comforted her, quelling the fear that had been rising in her since morning.

Grandpa came back and sat at the table. "He's going to make soup."

That would be good. It would go farther and seem like they were eating more than was really there. Miles played with disks, not caring what size rested on what.

Grandpa patted her hand. "The good Lord will provide another job."

"I hope it's soon." She recalled the look on Mr. MacGregor's face when she was fired. Why did he have to bear witness to her humility? "He stood there listening."

"Who, child?"

Had she said something aloud? "What?"

"You said, 'He stood there listening.' Who was listening to what?"

There was no sense in trying to evade his question. "Mr.

MacGregor had the audacity to stand in the doorway of his store while Miss Morgan terminated my employment."

"Who is this MacGregor?"

"The store owner next door. We've spoken from time to time as I arrive at work or when I'm leaving."

"Did he say something to you?"

At the thought of Mr. MacGregor's words, her humiliation burned anew. "He offered me money. I'm not some strumpet." She'd thought him a better man than that.

"Do you think his offer was less than honorable? Did he ask for anything in return?"

"I didn't give him the chance. I ran off. I always thought him a nice man." She put her face in her hands.

"Hmm."

As she lay in bed that night wondering how she would feed her family, a verse in James came to mind. *"Pure religion and undefiled before God and the Father is this, to visit the fatherless and widows in their affliction."* Yes, the church. They had to help her. She tithed faithfully, and now God was showing her how to get through this. He was providing for her until she could get another job. Tomorrow she would go and ask the minister for provisions.

❧

The following morning, Finn, a man about fifty with clothes more worn than her own, sat at Alice's table drinking a cup of coffee with Grandpa when she came out of her bedroom ready to search again for a job. Where had it come from? They hadn't been able to afford coffee in a very long time.

Grandpa raised his cup. "Finn brought it. Only enough for one pot, but it sure tastes good."

How long had it been? She poured a cup and savored the aroma.

"It's better if you drink it," Grandpa said.

She wrapped her hands around the warm cup. "I want to enjoy everything about it."

"Can I have some?" Burl asked.

She was about to refuse him when Grandpa nodded. "On one condition, young man. You be in school all day and pretend like you're learnin' somethin' and come home straightaway afterward. No dawdlin', no cuttin' shines with your friends."

Burl nodded. "I will." He turned to her. "I won't get in no more trouble. I promise. I learnt my lesson."

She poured Burl the last of the coffee, barely half a cup. He seemed earnest in his promise. Maybe the trouble with the ship's captain was worth losing her job if it straightened Burl out for good. *Lord, please help Burl hold fast to his conviction.*

Burl took a sip and grimaced. She hadn't liked coffee when she'd first tasted it, either, but it grew on her as it would Burl.

Grandpa pointed to Burl's cup. "Even if you don't finish that, you still have to keep our bargain."

Burl nodded and drank it down, then wiped his mouth with his sleeve. "That was good." He tried to sound grown-up.

"Off to school with you now." She smiled at his back. He was growing up, turning into a little man. A little man who would likely be taller than she was come summer.

She took a drink of her coffee and let the warm liquid sit in her mouth for a moment before swallowing it. *Thank You, Lord, for this treat.* "Finn, thank you for the coffee."

They didn't know much about Finn. He seemed to be a drifter. He wouldn't give any more name than Finn and wouldn't tell them where he lived. Probably in the train yard like so many bummers. He was a good friend to Grandpa, brought him the paper and kept him company a couple of days a week. Grandpa was sharing the Lord with him. Finn showed up when Finn wanted to, but always for Sunday dinner, and always with something to offer for the table—bread, biscuits, milk, potatoes. How he got the food, she couldn't imagine, and no one ever asked him. He and Grandpa had a deal. If Finn showed up for Sunday church service, he was welcome to Sunday dinner. Finn was faithfully at Sunday dinner.

She drank down her coffee, avoiding the grounds at the bottom. "I should be going. I have to move past Second and Third Streets, maybe all the way up to Sixth, searching."

"Hotel on Seventh might be needing a cleaning girl." Finn took a swig of his coffee. "If you want to go so far as the mill, the cook up there might be needing help. She cooks for a whole passel of men."

"Thank you, Finn." She hoped she didn't have to go that far and swung on her shawl.

"I think it was wrong for Miss Morgan to fire you." Finn turned his pale blue eyes on her.

"She has a business to run."

"Not very charitable for someone who sits in church every Sunday. She should know how important family is." He dipped his head down and mumbled. "Shouldn't have to learn the hard way."

What did Finn know about family? Maybe more than he let on. She sighed and headed out into the drizzle, dreading having to trudge through the muddy streets all day.

four

Alice sat by the fire of the stove late Friday night, finishing the mending she'd acquired that day. She strained to see where to make her stitches to keep them even. It wasn't steady employment, but it would feed them for a few days. If she finished and returned the garments in the morning, she could get paid and buy food. Her minister had given them half a dozen eggs, a small sack of flour, and a jar of canned tomatoes. She'd thanked him and God over and over for both the food and the mending job. Her minister was the one who had told her about the work.

Grandpa stepped into the pool of light. "You've done enough for tonight."

"I'm sorry for keeping you up. I'll be done soon."

"You work too hard."

"I have to."

Grandpa stood over her. "Even our heavenly Father rested. Not because He needed to but as an example to us all."

"As you know, He rested on the seventh day. It's not Sunday yet." She took another small stitch.

"I'm just saying you've worked hard today. You've earned your rest." Grandpa stifled a couple of coughs. He was not getting better.

She could not be idle for one minute if she was going to get him some better medicine. " 'In the morning sow thy seed, and in the evening withhold not thine hand: for thou knowest not whether thou shall prosper, either this or that, or whether they both shall be alike good.' I can't give up."

"It's not giving up to rest. Go to bed. You're going to wear yourself out."

"We only have enough food for tomorrow even with the charity. I need this work. 'If any would not work, neither should he eat.'"

"Don't you be spouting scripture to me, young lady." Grandpa shook his finger at her. "I taught you those verses."

"You taught me well."

Grandpa grumbled. "'Is not the life more than meat, and the body than raiment? Behold the fowls of the air: for they sow not, neither do they reap, nor gather into barns; yet your heavenly Father feedeth them. Are ye not much better than they?'"

She set the mending in her lap. "Are you insinuating that I'm not trusting God?"

Grandpa wagged his head back and forth. "All I'm saying is that you have worked hard, harder than most. You've done your part; now let God do His. Your hands have not been idle for one waking minute. God will reward you for your diligence. We will not go hungry."

She just wished there was food enough for more than one day and turned her focus back to her work. "I'll be done soon."

Grandpa stood in silence for a moment. "I think I'll go out tomorrow and get me a job."

She jerked her gaze up to him. "You'll do no such thing." His heart couldn't take the physical jobs available to an old man of his education.

"You won't be around to stop me. 'If any would not work, neither should he eat.'"

She'd meant that verse for herself. "Grandpa, please."

"I'd rather die doing something useful than sitting around here all day."

"Taking care of Miles for me is useful. I couldn't work if I didn't know you were here with him. I daresay Miles likely affords you little time to sit."

"Burl could care for him. He's old enough."

She lowered her voice. "What if he goes off on one of his troublemaking schemes and leaves Miles here alone? Or worse yet, takes him with him?" She didn't need Miles trained in cutting shines and making mischief before he even started school.

"He wouldn't do that. He only gets in trouble because he doesn't want to be in school."

"Maybe so, but I'd feel better with you here with Miles."

A cough rattled inside Grandpa's chest. "There's going to come a time when I won't be around anymore and the task will fall to Burl."

"Don't say that." She looked away from him.

"We've both been thinking it. One less mouth to feed would be easier on you."

"No." Tears clouded her vision.

"What man lives well into his seventies and sees his great-grandchild born? I've had a good life, but it's comin' to an end. You need to face that."

She didn't want to think about it. "We're managing. We have the food from the minister, and I'll get money for this mending. We'll make do. I just wish we had a small garden; then at least we'd always have a few vegetables."

Grandpa coughed. "Maybe I could build you a potting box. Put it here under the window and grow a couple of tomato plants."

She held the mending to her thighs as she stood and hugged Grandpa. "That would be wonderful." She knew he wouldn't be able to with having only one hand and his joints hurting him so, but he never complained about his hardships. And neither would she complain about hers.

"I'll only do it if you go to bed right now."

She set her mending aside—she could finish it first thing in the morning—and gave Grandpa a kiss on the cheek. "I love you."

"I love you, too. Now scoot."

She closed herself in her room and leaned against the door. *Lord, I know he is old, but don't take him from me yet. I wouldn't be able to bear up under it.*

⋅ ❧

As Ian was giving Mr. Baker instructions on his medicine, two elderly men entered his store. The pair had their heads together, whispering, and pointed toward him and Conner. He tapped Conner on the arm and inclined his head toward them. Conner immediately went over, leaving him to finish up with Mr. Baker.

"No, thank you. My business is with Mr. MacGregor," the older of the two men said then issued a chest-rattling cough.

Ian saw Mr. Baker to the door and went to the two men.

Conner said, "These gentlemen want to talk only to you."

He removed his glasses. "How may I help you?" Something for that cough no doubt.

The older man held out his hand. "Arthur Greig."

He shook it. The man's Scottish brogue tickled his ears. "Ian MacGregor, proprietor. What can I do for you?"

The smaller man pointed at him. "We want to know what your intentions are toward his granddaughter."

He looked from the smaller man to Mr. Greig and searched his memory for any young lady with the last name Greig. "I don't believe I'm familiar with your granddaughter."

"Ha. He's going to deny it."

"Finn, calm down." Mr. Greig squared his shoulders.

That action looked familiar. But from where?

"My granddaughter is Alice Dempsey. Until a few days ago, she worked at the millinery shop next door."

He should have guessed Mr. Greig was talking about Alice. She straightened her shoulders just like her grandfather. "Yes, I'm acquainted with Miss Dempsey. I was sorry she lost her position next door. Is she doing well? Has she acquired a new position?" Well maybe the Lord hadn't sent Miss Dempsey through his door, but Ian was going to get as much information from her grandfather as the man would allow.

"She's doing well but hasn't found much work yet."

"I'm sorry to hear that," Ian said and meant it. "Maybe I can help her find employment."

"That is not why I came." Mr. Greig narrowed his gaze. "Did you or did you not offer my granddaughter money?"

"She's not a strumpet, you know!" Finn threw in.

Oh dear. He knew that had been the worst thing he could have said to Alice the moment it passed his lips. "Mr. Greig, please believe me, I meant no disrespect to your granddaughter. I was only trying to help. She seemed quite distressed about her fix. I wanted her to know that she had a friend to turn to if she needed help. The money offer was to help her along until she secured another position." He likely would have given her his whole wallet at the time. He remembered a saying of his grandmother's, *A fool and his money are soon parted.* He was no fool. . .or at least he wouldn't be again.

Mr. Greig took in a deep breath and had a fit of coughs.

"That is a nasty cough you have." He guided the man to a chair in the back. "Please sit."

Conner brought a glass of water.

Mr. Greig drank. "So exactly what are your intentions toward my granddaughter?"

Ian looked to Conner, who gave him an encouraging nod.

"I'd like to help her—all of you—in any way I can."

"You'd be wanting somethin' in return for that help, I reckon." Finn curled up his lip.

"Of course not." He gave his attention back to Mr. Greig. "My intentions toward your granddaughter are honorable."

Conner stepped forward. "What he's trying to say is that—"

"What I'm trying to say is that I've been sweet on your granddaughter for some time."

"And. . . ," Conner encouraged.

"And with your permission, I'd like to court her."

Conner slapped him on the back. "You won't find a finer

gentleman than Ian here." The bell over the door jingled. "I'll get that."

Mr. Greig eyed him for a moment. "You come over tomorrow for Sunday dinner, and we'll see about the courting."

He smiled, hope springing up in him. "I'd be honored." Did Alice know her grandfather was here? Had she sent him? "Where?"

Finn spoke up, "You know the bank on Third?"

He nodded.

"Meet me there, and I'll take you over."

Mr. Greig stood to leave and started coughing. Finn handed him his glass of water.

Ian went to one of his medicine shelves and brought back a jar of red mustard and skunk oil. "Rub this poultice into your chest. You'll cough up whatever you have in there, but then you should feel better and be able to sleep."

Mr. Greig waved it away. "Can't pay."

"I didn't ask you to." He slipped it into the old man's pocket then turned to Finn. "He should go home and rest."

"That's like puttin' a hurry on the city to finish these streets and make the upper sidewalks, but I'll try." Finn put his arm around the older man.

Mr. Greig waved him off. "I'm not an invalid, Finn. Least ways not yet."

As the two men reached the door, Ian grabbed a pouch of wild cherry bark and bloodroot. "Finn." The man turned, and he tossed him the bag. "Brew that into a tea and have him drink it as hot as he can stand."

Finn pocketed the pouch and nodded. Before the door closed behind the men, Ian heard Finn say, "I like him."

"Well, it looks like you won Finn over." Conner stepped around from behind the counter.

"It's not Finn or Mr. Greig I'm concerned about winning over. It's Miss Dempsey."

"I prayed for Miss Dempsey to cross your threshold; I

guess her grandfather is close enough."

Ian stared at the door. "Just because he came here doesn't mean she ever will."

"No, you're going to her house, which is better. When are you ever going to believe in yourself? If the grandfather likes you, you have half the battle fought and won."

"The grandfather's friend liked me, and I have won nothing."

Conner smiled. "But you will."

&

On Sunday after church, Alice put the noodles she'd made into the pot of boiling water. She would cut up the pork bacon and two carrots to put in as well. They would be eating like royalty today. Her mending job had afforded them a few days' food. But tomorrow she must find a job.

Grandpa went to the window again and looked out. What was with him pacing? He was never so unsettled.

"Are you feeling well?"

"Fine, child, fine."

"Well, sit down. You're making me nervous." She waved him toward the table.

"Finn should have been here by now. I'll just go see what's keeping him."

At least that would keep him from worrying a hole clean through her floor. "Don't forget your coat." Finn usually came straight home with them from church but today said he had something to do first.

Burl hooked his thumbs chest high into his gallows. "I'm goin', too."

"You stay put." Grandpa put on his coat.

"Ah, Grandpa." Burl slouched. "I wanna come."

"You stay and help your sister."

"I wanna go with you."

"Not this time, son. I'll be back before you know it. Finn's probably climbing the stairs as we speak." Grandpa slipped out the door before Burl could protest further.

Burl slumped into a chair and folded his arms. Miles lay on Grandpa and Burl's mattress, napping. He was always tired after church.

Once the carrots were soft and the noodles cooked, Alice put the chopped-up bacon into the soup pot and then heard the door open.

"We have company for dinner," Grandpa called.

Without turning from the stove, she said, "Welcome, Finn."

"Lass, don't be rude. Greet our guests."

She turned from the stove. The breath froze in her chest. Mr. MacGregor stood hat in hand between Grandpa and Finn.

Finn jabbed his thumb toward Mr. MacGregor. "Look who we found on the corner."

Found indeed.

Mr. MacGregor took a step forward. "I hope I'm not intruding. Mr. Greig invited me."

She looked from Mr. MacGregor to Grandpa and back. She released her captive breath. "You are welcome in our humble home and to eat at our table."

Finn handed her a loaf of bread, no doubt stale but none the less filling. Dipped in the soup, it would be tasty. Would Mr. MacGregor think their meal pitiful? She wished she had more to offer him.

Mr. MacGregor handed her a paper bag of Saratoga potato chips. "I didn't know what you were fixing. I figured these would go with anything." His eyes begged forgiveness.

But for what? Coming unannounced or for having to set foot in her tenement apartment? "Thank you." He would see her differently now. And probably for the last time. An ache knotted inside her.

She motioned toward Burl. "This is my brother, Burl."

Mr. MacGregor held out his hand to Burl. "I hear you

almost set sail on the high seas."

Burl squared his shoulders and shook his hand. "No, sir. I'll be stayin' on land."

"Then you'll be staying away from the docks?"

"Yes, sir."

Miles started crying. "Ma."

She went to him and held him. He often got scared when he first woke up. She stood and adjusted him on her hip. "This is my son, Miles."

Mr. MacGregor stared at her child for a moment, clearly surprised. "It's good to meet you, little man."

Miles wedged his face into her neck.

"Miles, say good day to our guest."

"Good day," came his muffled voice from her neck.

Yes, this would be the last any of them would see of Mr. MacGregor. She felt her lower lip begin to quiver. "I'll just finish getting dinner ready." She turned back to the stove with tears in her eyes. He wouldn't be looking at her the same. Gone would be the image of the pretty young lady and in its place the mother with no husband living in a little apartment in the shoddy part of town. It was one thing to have Finn, a drifter, in their home, another to have an upstanding man like Mr. MacGregor. Why did she even care what he thought of her? She shouldn't. She didn't.

"What kind of store do you got?" Burl asked.

"Burl, don't be rude," Grandpa said.

"I don't mind. I own a pharmacy."

"Really? What do you got in there?" Burl continued to ask questions, and Mr. MacGregor patiently answered every one of them.

Alice stirred the soup, putting off facing Mr. MacGregor at her table. He must think them below his station. She was surprised he hadn't excused himself and left already. Miles wiggled out of her arm and ran over to the table where the men all sat. He evidently had become comfortable with the stranger in the house. She wrapped a towel around the handle of the soup kettle and carried it to the table. "Soup's ready."

All the men stood, including Burl.

"Burl, you and Miles can sit over by the stove if you like."

"I wanna sit at the table." Burl looked up at Mr. MacGregor.

She didn't want to draw attention to the fact that they didn't have enough chairs for everyone.

Grandpa gave him a stern look. "Do as your sister says. You two can sit on the edge of the mattress."

Miles ran over and sat on the straw-filled ticking. That was a treat, even if it wasn't much softer than the floor.

Grandpa stood at the head of the table and motioned for the others to join him.

Mr. MacGregor was at the seat with the crate. She couldn't have that. She grabbed the crate before anyone sat. "I'll sit on this."

Mr. MacGregor grabbed the other side of the crate. "I don't mind."

She couldn't let a guest use it. "Please, you'll be more comfortable in the chair. I insist."

"This is not a proper seat for a lady. I insist." He pulled the crate.

A sharp pain stabbed at her finger, and she released the crate with a gasp, three slivers in her middle finger and one in her index.

"Oh dear. What have I done?" Mr. MacGregor set the crate down. "Let me take a look."

She squeezed her finger. "I'll be fine." They weren't too bad. Most of the ends were sticking out a fraction, so she should be able to pull them out later.

He grabbed her wrist and pulled her along to the window, where there was better light. "I can get these. Do you have a needle?"

"Burl, get Alice's sewing basket," Grandpa ordered.

"Really, I'll be fine." She wanted to pull her hand from his grasp but didn't for some reason. His hand was strong and warm.

He released her hand to pull out a pocketknife and opened it. This was her chance to get away. She stood motionless.

Burl brought the sewing basket.

"Find me a needle."

Burl did as Mr. MacGregor commanded.

Mr. MacGregor slipped the blade of his knife under the end of the largest sliver and pressed his thumb against it, then slowly pulled it out. He squeezed her finger, forcing blood out. "That will help clean the wound." He wiped away the blood with his thumb and attacked the other slivers. He worked gently, using the needle to pull up the ends, and then pulled them out. No broken ends left under her skin to fester. He concentrated so deeply on his work, she doubted he even realized he was holding her hand.

He worked the last sliver out and looked up to her face. "There. Those won't give you any more trouble." He glanced back down at their hands together and jerked his away. "Sorry," he whispered, ducking his head.

Her hand cooled quickly where he'd held it. "Thank you."

He gave her a smile and gazed deep into her eyes. Was he trying to look into her soul? Or change her feelings?

She broke his stare and went to the table. She would not and could not fancy thoughts of Mr. MacGregor. She could not let Mr. MacGregor fancy thoughts of her, either. It was good that he had come and seen their humble dwelling. He would see now that his affections were better directed elsewhere.

Grandpa blessed the food and thanked the Lord for friends to share it with. "Smells real good, Granddaughter."

It did smell good, but she wasn't hungry anymore.

five

"Thank you, Mrs. Dempsey. It was a very delicious meal." *Mrs.* felt like sand in Ian's mouth. He knew it shouldn't; she was a widow. But did she still mourn her loss? Did she still love him? Did her heart ache for him every time she looked at her son? Did she wish she could go back to when he was still alive?

"Mr. MacGregor?"

Ian turned his focus to Mr. Greig, who still had a hint of his Scottish accent. He savored it. It made him homesick for his parents. "Please call me Ian."

"Very well, lad. Did you know that Greig is a sept of the clan MacGregor?"

"No, sir, I did not."

Mr. Greig went to an old chest and pulled out a dominantly red tartan. "Our families are connected in the old country."

He fingered the familiar plaid. "It seems so, sir."

"You have no accent."

"I was a wee babe when my folks came over from Scotland." He put on his parents' familiar accent. "Your accent is like going home. 'Tis very comforting, indeed."

Mr. Greig nodded. He seemed to like Ian's comment and accent.

"Do you speak Gaelic?"

In Gaelic, Mr. Greig said, "I do."

Ian replied in kind. "My parents taught me as well." He bantered for a minute with Mr. Greig then asked, "Did the treatment I gave you help?"

"Aye. I haven't slept so well since. . .in a very long time."

He noticed Alice glaring at her grandfather, so he switched

back to English. "I'm glad to hear it."

"Your Gaelic is very good." Mr. Greig switched back to English as well.

Miles appeared at the side of his. . .crate, staring up at him. He smiled down at the tot. "Hello."

Miles studied him for a moment then raised his hands to him.

He wasn't sure what the child wanted but reached under his arms and lifted him onto his lap. Now what?

"Miles, get down." Mrs. Dempsey started to rise.

"It's all right. I don't mind."

She settled back into her chair but looked a little nervous at his holding her child.

After the meal, Ian took advantage of Miss—Mrs. Dempsey's being alone in the kitchen area and carried over the soup pot. "Where should I put this?"

"You didn't have to carry that over."

"It was no trouble."

She pointed. "Set it back on the stove, and I'll wash it in a bit."

"I wanted to thank you again for dinner. It was very good. You are a good cook." He was avoiding what he really wanted to say, or rather ask.

"Thank you." She dipped her head as though embarrassed.

"Honestly. It was delicious."

She squared her shoulders. "You didn't eat much. I thought you didn't like it."

"It was tasty. And I enjoyed every bite." He'd purposefully not eaten as much as he would normally to make sure there was plenty for the others, especially the children. Burl had kept eating until every crumb was gone. He wished he'd brought something more substantial to the table than potato chips. He'd thought they would be fun and Burl would enjoy them.

"When I find employment, I'll pay you for the medicine you gave Grandpa."

"You understand Gaelic?"

"Grandpa and my mama used to speak it all the time. He wouldn't tell me where he got the tea and poultice. I assumed it was from Finn. He's always showing up with unusual things." She paused. "I'll pay you back."

"That is not necessary. It was the Christian thing to do."

"But I will—"

"I won't accept it. They were a gift. I didn't come over here to argue with you. I came to ask you to come work for me."

She spun and pinned him with her slightly narrowed eyes. "I don't think that will do." She seemed agitated, but he didn't know why.

"You've found a position then?"

"No, but. . ." She collected the spoons and turned them around in her hands. "I—I know nothing of working with medicine."

"You wouldn't be working with the drugs directly. I'd be doing that. There are many other tasks to be done. My assistant, Conner, will not be staying with me forever. He has dreams of his own business."

Miles came over and held up his hands. "Ma."

She picked up the child.

He gazed at her, willing her to accept his offer, to accept him.

She looked away. "Thank you for your offer, but I don't think I could do it. I'm not skilled for that kind of work." There was a quaver in her voice.

Should he insist or let it go? Before he could decide, a hand clamped onto his shoulder. He turned to face Mr. Greig.

"Let me walk you out."

Was he being kicked out?

"Mrs. Dempsey, thank you once again for dinner." He turned and followed the old men to the door.

Burl jumped up from where he sat on the floor. "Can I go?"

Mr. Greig must have given the boy some kind of look Ian couldn't see, because Burl sat back down.

He took the stairs slowly and helped to support Mr. Greig. Once outside, Finn excused himself and ambled on down the street.

When Mr. Greig shuffled his feet to start walking. Ian stepped in front of him to block his progress and smiled. "Let's not pretend you really want to take a stroll. You shouldn't be out in this damp cold. You must have something important to say to me in private."

Mr. Greig chuckled. "You're more perceptive than I give most folks credit."

He nodded. His grandmother always said he had a special insight about things like that. It wasn't infallible, but he was usually dead on, and it helped him in discerning what his customers needed. If it only would help him where Alice was concerned. "It didn't go so well up there."

"It went better than I had hoped."

The older man obviously had a different idea of success than he did. He'd had hopes that this dinner would be the start of a relationship with Alice, but instead, she didn't seem to want him around and certainly didn't want his job offer. "You wanted me to make a fool of myself?"

"You are no fool."

"I certainly didn't impress anyone."

"You impressed me."

He didn't see how. "Was it my staring at her son like an imbecile? Or when I fought for the crate and injured her?"

"Actually both. I wasn't sure if you knew about Burl or Miles. You knew about Burl from Mr. Jackson, but Miles was a surprise to you. You rose to the occasion. I was impressed when you let Miles on your lap."

"He's a cute little tyke." He wanted desperately to ask about Mr. Dempsey. "And how could my stealing the crate from your granddaughter and injuring her impress you?"

"You were trying to be a gentleman and let Alice have the better seat, but she was less than cooperative. The slivers were her own doing, but you made sure her hand was properly cared for."

Amazing. He'd actually made a good impression on Mr. Greig even with his fumbling through the meal. "I don't think"—he didn't want to say *missus* aloud again—"your granddaughter saw any of it that way."

"That's what I wanted to talk to you about. What I'm about to tell you stays between the two of us. Don't ever tell Alice I spilled the beans."

Ian nodded his consent.

"Alice's husband was a bad egg. He charmed her, and I'm sorry to say that he charmed me as well. Soon after they were married, he began to show himself for who he truly was. By then it was too late, and Alice was with child. He gambled and drank away everything we had."

Ian wasn't sure why Mr. Greig was telling him, but he had to know. "What happened to him?"

"He cheated in a card game and was shot and killed, but by then we had nothing left and had to leave the farm I had worked hard to pay for when I first came to the area. She feels responsible for us losing it all. It wasn't her fault. Oscar had two faces. He showed us the one we wanted to see. I should have recognized it from the start."

"So she's not still mourning his passing?" The bold question was out before he could stop it, but he wasn't sorry he'd asked. He needed to know where Alice's heart lay.

"If she wasn't a Christian, she'd be cursing him every day. She doesn't talk about him or let anyone else talk about him. She mourns the loss of my farm."

Ian's heart went out to Alice for the life she had lost because of her husband and the life she now endured because of him. She had suffered much at such a young age but stood proud and strong. He wanted to take away all her hardships and pain. "Why have you confided all this to me?"

"If you're interested in courting my granddaughter, I want

you to know. Now that you do and have seen how we live, you may not be so interested."

"I am more interested. Before she was little more than a beautiful woman to me. When I spoke to her, I knew she was sweet and seemed gentle. Now I–I'm in awe. She works so hard to put food on the table for all of you and a roof over your heads." Words could not convey his feelings and respect for Alice.

"I'd help if I could." Mr. Greig held up his stump arm. "This old body's giving out on me."

"She wouldn't want you to." He paused. "I offered her a job."

"She turned you down."

"You heard."

Mr. Greig shook his head. "She doesn't want to be beholden to any man ever again. Knows you are different from other employers who are men. Whether she will admit it or not, she knows you have feelings for her. She won't give in to that easily. Her stubborn Scottish pride. You'd have a better chance of her inviting you over for supper than her accepting your job offer."

Why? It didn't have to be that way. "I just want to help."

"She's been hurt real bad. She'll need a lot of patience." Mr. Greig thumped his fist on his chest and coughed.

"You'd better get inside. Make some of that tea, rub the ointment on your chest, and rest. I'll come by later in the week to see how you're doing."

"And to see Alice."

He had to smile. "Good day, Mr. Greig."

"Call me Arthur." The old man shook his hand then went inside.

He followed him in and helped him up the stairs.

Arthur smiled and spoke in Gaelic. "You are a good man."

He thanked him in Gaelic and left. Instead of heading home, Ian went to his store in hopes of talking to Conner.

The door was locked and the inside was dark. Conner must have gone out. He walked around the store to see all that the Lord had blessed him with. Far more than Mrs. Dempsey and her family. He moved a jar. There was enough dirt and dust behind it to grow a small garden. This would be a job that Mrs. Dempsey could do. Neither he nor Conner had the time to do this work.

He walked into the storeroom that was not Conner's living quarters. The crate with the medicines from Captain Carlyle's ship sat unopened. He'd told Conner to leave it for him, that he would unpack it. Conner was very conscientious when it came to the drugs he sold.

He searched for the crowbar to pry off the top of the crate. A rat scurried from behind an empty crate, rose up on his haunches, and scolded him with a raspy squeak.

"There you are. I'm going to get you once and for all." With one eye on the pest, he grabbed a broom and took a step.

The beady-eyed rodent darted down and ran for the darkest corner.

He gave chase, knocking over empty crates and bruising his foot on a heavy one in his haste. He jammed the broom into the corner and pushed boxes out of the way. There was no way it was getting away this time. He ran around the room, tipping over empty crates. He cornered it behind a packing keg, aimed his weapon, and lunged.

It squealed and darted between his legs.

Spinning around, he came face-to-face with Conner holding a raised board in his hand.

Conner gasped. "You scared the tar out of me! I thought someone had broken in, except a thief wouldn't be making so much noise."

"I was trying to get the fool rat."

"You mean Vern."

He scowled. "You named it?"

"I've been trying to trap him for weeks. He's smarter than

two rats combined. He gets the bait without springing the trap."

"So you named it?"

"I was trying to make friends with him, get him to trust me. Then just when he was feeling safe—*bam!*" Conner slammed a fist into his palm. "I'd grab him."

"Is it working?"

Conner shook his head. "He's too smart for that."

He sighed. "So how are we going to get rid of him?"

Conner smiled and held up a finger. "I have just the thing. I'm done being nice."

Ian followed Conner out into the main part of the store. Tied up by the door sat a little brown dog with muddy fur and a yellow puddle on the floor next to it.

"I'll take care of that." Conner picked up the scruffy dog. "Terriers are good ratters. Within a week, we'll no longer have a rat problem."

"I hope so." He scratched the dog behind the ear, and it licked his hand. "Does he have a name?"

"She. I've named her Fred."

He raised an eyebrow. "For a girl?"

Conner shrugged. "Sure. She seems to like it." He looked down at the dog. "Don't you, Fred?" Fred tipped her head back and licked his chin.

"Where did you get a mongrel like her?"

"Most people see a useless mongrel, but I don't think so. She needs a home, and we need one less rat in this store. Let's see if she can sniff out our little problem." He set the dog on the floor inside the storeroom. "Can you smell it, girl? Go get Vern."

Fred looked up at him, whined, and sat on Conner's boot.

"I'll train her."

"Are you also going to give her a bath?" The dog was cute but had a bit of an odor about her.

"I'll take care of her. I hear tell the city is paying ten cents a dead rat. Just bring 'em the tail. Before long, Fred'll be able to earn her keep." He picked up the dog, scratching her behind the ear. "Since we aren't open and you don't usually come in on Sundays, I will assume you came from Miss Dempsey's. How did it go?"

Ian groaned thinking about the fiasco. "I felt like a log sliding in the mud down Skid Road toward the frigid waters of Puget Sound."

"That bad?"

"Mr. Greig failed to warn his granddaughter I was coming." He figured that was a calculated move on Arthur's part, but he wasn't sure if it was to see Ian's reaction or to avoid giving his granddaughter a chance to bow out of the meal.

"Was she mad?" Conner shifted Fred to his other arm.

"If she was, she hid it well. She was surprised and a little flustered. I, on the other hand, behaved wretchedly. Her grandfather's friend was there—"

"That's good. He liked you."

A small consolation. "I met her brother, Burl."

"He's kind of a cute kid. Did you get on well with him?"

"He asked a lot of questions about my business. He seemed real interested."

"It sounds as though things went well. I don't see any problems."

Ian leaned on the broom he still held. "Then she introduced me to her three-year-old son, Miles." He'd never imagined her with a child. Now he couldn't picture her without him.

Conner's brown eyes widened. "She's married?"

"Widowed." But he couldn't tell Conner that whole story.

Conner raised an eyebrow. "You don't have a problem with that, do you?"

"No. But I just stared at her child as though he were a raccoon or something. It was so unexpected, I didn't know what to say."

"After that you improved, right?"

"Until we sat down to eat, or tried to sit down. We fought over who was going to sit on the crate. She wanted her guests and her grandfather to have the three chairs. As a gentleman, I couldn't let her sit on the crate." Some gentleman he'd been.

Conner was grimacing. "Who won?"

"No one. I ended up taking the crate from her. Gave her four slivers in her fingers, but I forcibly removed them." He gave Conner a wry smile.

"Forcibly?"

"She didn't want me to." He poked his chest with his thumbs. "But I insisted. Then at the table, her grandfather and I started speaking in Gaelic, excluding everyone else. She wasn't too happy about that."

"The time was not wasted entirely. The grandfather likes you now, his friend likes you, and it sounds like Burl likes you. How did her son react?"

"Shy at first; then he climbed into my lap." The boy was adorable and looked like his mother. He was glad of that. To look at Miles and see characteristics that would have to be attributed to the child's no-good father would be hard.

"It sounds like you won everyone over."

"Except Mrs. Dempsey." He sighed. "I offered her a job."

"Are you planning on getting rid of me soon?"

"If I could keep you in my employ indefinitely, I would, but I know you have plans of your own that will take you beyond Seattle. You've incorporated some good ideas into the store. You'll do well in your own business one day. I have money enough to support two employees. Have you seen the dirt and dust on the back of some of those shelves?"

Conner rubbed the back of his neck. "I've been meaning to get to that."

"It's a job Alice could easily do." He finally leaned the broom against the storage room wall and stepped out of the room.

Fred wiggled, and Conner set her on the floor. "Will she be in tomorrow?"

He shook his head. "She turned it down."

"Did she find another position?"

"No. She just doesn't want to work for me." And he couldn't understand why when she needed a job. Her husband's betrayal must have cut deep.

"If she doesn't find another job, she'll come here." Conner gave him an encouraging nod.

"I wouldn't count on that."

"Maybe the grandfather will talk sense into her. You could speak to him." Conner filled a bucket with water and grabbed a couple of rags and headed for Fred's accident by the front door.

He would wait a couple of days then he would speak to Arthur. Arthur might be able to talk her into it, help her see the logic in it.

six

Alice pulled her crocheted shawl closer, covering the bundle she held tight to her chest, then stepped out into the pouring rain. Her straw hat afforded her little protection. It had rained steadily for three days and off and on for three weeks. The ground couldn't soak up any more water.

She dipped her head and scurried through the mud. She came to a puddle that spanned the street and was fifty feet long. She knew this was a low point. It often pooled but not usually to this extent. A boy of about nine, sitting on a crude raft of large sticks, paddled his way across the murky water. That was not an option for her. She went a block up, dodging several smaller puddles still substantial in their own right.

She wound her way to the street she was looking for. The looming edifice of the mansion was more intimidating this time than the last time she was here. She felt small and wanted to turn back, but she knew she couldn't. They'd eaten the last of the food for breakfast. She'd worked late into the night to finish this new sewing the minister had directed her toward so she'd have money to buy food.

Brick and columns greeted her, but she knew enough not to dare enter that way. She hurried around back and knocked on the kitchen door.

A tall woman with a big frame and fading blond hair opened the door. "Mercy, child, come in. You'll catch your death out there."

She stepped inside, dripping and shivering. January rains were the coldest. "I brought Mrs. Rush's sewing." Her teeth clicked against each other.

"What are you doing out on a day like this? You'll catch

your death." The woman wiped her hands on her white apron. "Come stand by the stove."

She shook her head. "I don't want to dirty up your kitchen."

"Fiddlesticks." The woman took her by the arm and drew her toward the warmth. She took the package wrapped in soggy brown paper and set it on the table. Next she took Alice's shawl and short jacket. "Don't you move from that stove. I'll be right back."

She huddled as close to the stove as she could without getting burned. *Lord, please protect my health. I can't afford to get sick.*

The woman returned. "It'll just be a moment. I'm Marjorie."

"Alice." Her teeth had stopped chattering.

Marjorie poured a cup of coffee and handed it to her. "This'll warm you up from the inside."

Alice wrapped her hands around the warm china and sipped the brew. This was the second time in less than a week. "Thank you."

A woman with graying black hair came in. "I'm Sally. What's your business here?"

"I brought Mrs. Rush's sewing. I finished it right up and brought it straightaway."

Sally and Marjorie exchanged a look. Sally pointed to the soggy bundle on the table. "Let me see what you did for her."

Alice spread out the walking suit and showed Sally where she'd repaired the hem and reattached the three buttons. Then she showed her the blouses. "Mrs. Rush gave me fabric to make a blouse just like this one."

Sally smiled in a sad way. "You do fine work." She scooped up the clothes. "Stay here while I go see Mrs. Rush." She turned to Marjorie. "Get her some tea."

"I already poured her coffee."

"Then get her a biscuit and open a jar of apple butter." Sally left through the swinging door.

Neither Sally nor Marjorie had been there when she'd

come before. Whether it was their day off or they were out running errands she couldn't say, but she was glad for their hospitality now.

Marjorie set a china plate with a biscuit on the table. "Sit." Then she popped open a fresh jar and set it on the table.

How long had it been since she'd had apple butter? She opened her biscuit and spread a thin layer of preserve on it, then just stared at it. How could she indulge while her family went without?

Marjorie sat with a cup of coffee in her hand. "Is there something wrong, dear?"

She shook her head. "I was just wondering how long it's been since I've had apple butter." Or any preserves.

Marjorie dipped the knife into the jar then slathered a glop of apple butter on Alice's biscuit. She smiled. "Enjoy."

She would not turn away food that the Lord had put in her hand. The apple butter was sweet and cinnamony in her mouth. Better than she remembered.

"I made that myself."

"It's delicious."

Marjorie's face beamed then quickly lost its cheerfulness when a loud, scratchy voice invaded the kitchen from the other room.

"They are all wet!"

Alice could feel her insides tighten and set her half-eaten biscuit back onto the plate.

Murmurs came through the door then, "This work is no good!"

The near screech pierced her heart.

More murmurs.

Soon Sally came back through the kitchen door with a scowl, shaking her head. "Nothing pleases that woman."

Marjorie stood. "Not again. When mean was being handed out, she stood in line twice."

"Marjorie." Sally gave the younger woman a stern look.

"You're right. I'm sorry. She stood in line ten times."

Sally only sighed then turned toward Alice. "I'm sorry. She's a stiff-necked woman who doesn't like anything or anyone."

Marjorie craned her neck to look up at Sally standing near to her. "And you're just going to let it go at that?"

"What else can I do?" Sally sighed again.

"Nothing, I suppose." Marjorie stood. "But I can do something." She took up an empty flour sack, and in went a loaf of bread.

While Marjorie flitted about the kitchen, she looked up at Sally. She didn't want to voice her fear but had to. "She's not going to pay me?"

Sally sat down and patted Alice's hand. "Best advice I can give you is if Mrs. Rush ever asks you to sew for her again, turn her down."

"But I was counting on that money to buy food. I lost my job and need to feed my family." What would she do now?

Marjorie set the bulging flour sack in front of her. "Here you go, sweetie. Feed your family."

What was this?

Sally's eyes widened. "Mrs. Rush will fire you if she finds out."

"So be it. I'm real tired of her cheatin' people." Marjorie picked up the sack and set it on the floor, then set it back on the table. "This food's been on the floor. Mrs. Rush won't want it."

What were they doing?

Sally smiled. "We'll have to throw it out anyway."

Marjorie twisted the lid back on the apple butter. "I think this jar is spoiled. It didn't taste very good." She opened the sack and put the jar inside.

Alice stared at the woman. "The apple butter tasted fine to me."

Sally straightened her smile. "No. If Marjorie says it's no good, then we have to throw it out. We'll not serve Mrs.

Rush any food that's no good." Her face softened, and kindness filled her eyes. "Take the food."

They were giving her food from Mrs. Rush's pantry? Her family would be able to eat. She wanted to grab the food and run out the door. But was it theirs to give? "I couldn't."

"It's not charity." Sally folded down the top of the bag and held it out to her. "You earned every last bite."

She hugged the bag to her chest. "Thank you." Then she put on her jacket and shawl. She wanted to cry at the treasure they'd given her.

Sally shook her head. "Is that all you got for this kind of weather?"

She pulled the shawl tighter. "I'll be fine."

"Fiddlesticks. Fine indeed." Sally disappeared into a back room then reappeared with an old coat, obviously for a man. "It's not fashionable, but it will keep the rain off you."

"I can't take this," Alice said as the two dressed her in the coat.

"You can and you will."

Marjorie draped Alice's shawl over her hat and tied a lumpy knot under her chin. The stove had half dried it. "Go the long way around the drive so as Mrs. Rush don't see that bag."

"I don't want you two to get into trouble."

"We'll be fine. She wouldn't dare fire us. She'd never find anyone else to work for her as long as we have." Sally smiled. "You go now."

"And stay warm," Marjorie called after her.

She was warm on the inside from their kindness and generosity. *Thank You, Lord, for sending me into the arms of those two kind women. Please don't let them get into any trouble on my account. And bless them a hundredfold for their kindness.*

The food tucked inside the coat weighed on her like a burden. She wanted the food, desperately so. She needed the food, but she didn't want what seemed like a blessing to turn into a curse because of dishonorable actions. She stopped under the bare arms of a huge, ancient tree on the far side of the drive and leaned against the trunk. She felt like this tree, stripped bare.

Lord, should I keep this food or take it back?

She heard Sally's voice tumble through her head, *"You earned every last bite."*

She had done honest work for the woman.

Give us day by day our daily bread.

She'd prayed for the Lord to provide food for her family. She'd expected it to be in the form of a permanent job so she could purchase food. *Daily bread.* The Lord had done just that, provided them food day by day. They'd not yet gone hungry.

Thank You, Lord. Please keep food in our stomachs and our hearts full of gratitude. She ducked her head to the rain and set her feet toward home.

❧

Tuesday night, Alice sat on the floor with a single candle burning in front of her and her skirt draped over her crossed legs. She took small stitches, careful to make the vertical tear look like a seam. This was the best skirt she had. She had to keep it in good order if she was going to find a decent job. Who would want to hire her if she looked like an ill-kept guttersnipe?

A verse from 1 Timothy came to her mind. *"Now she that is a widow indeed, and desolate, trusteth in God, and continueth in supplications and prayers night and day."* She was indeed a widow and desolate. *God in heaven who watches over the meek and weary, You have always looked out for widows, orphans, and the poor. We are all of those, and You have taken care of us. But my faith is growing weak. I can't go on like this much longer. I desperately need a job, or we will all starve. I don't know how much more the church can afford to give us. To be honest, I just want to give up, but I know I can't. Just for tonight, I'll give up, and in the morning, I'll go back to being strong and searching for a job.*

She sighed and leaned her head against the wall. Maybe she

should reconsider taking the position with Mr. MacGregor. He was a nice man. But that was exactly why she wouldn't take the position with him. She didn't want to find out that he would use her poor circumstances to take advantage of her. He was a nice man, and she didn't want to think of him any other way. No, she would not work for him. At least not for another day.

Her door squeaked slightly, and she looked up. "Come in, Burl," she whispered and glanced at Miles sleeping snuggled under the threadbare quilt.

Burl sat on the floor next to her. "I saw the light."

"Couldn't you sleep?"

He shook his head. "What're you doin'?"

"Mending my skirt. I have to look good when I talk to prospective employers."

Burl lowered his head. "You ain't never had this much trouble findin' a new job before. I'm sorry for losin' you your job."

She should scold him again and remind him that what one soweth that shall they reap. Actions did not go without consequences. It was a lesson he had yet to learn, one he insisted on beating his head against repeatedly. Would one more talking-to finally get through to him? She was too tired tonight to go rounds with him, so she wrapped an arm around his slim shoulders. "Don't you worry about that. The Lord has a position out there waiting for me. I just haven't found it yet. It's probably a much better job. We'll be fine."

"I'm gonna quit schoolin' and find me a job. Help out like a real man."

"No you won't. We don't have land to farm anymore. You need schooling to get a good job when you're older. I don't want you working your life away in a factory." It would be such a waste of his intelligence. "You are staying in school. I don't want to hear any more talk of quitting. The Lord will take care of us. We have to believe that."

"He's not doin' a very good job."

"Burl, don't say that. We still have a roof over our heads and food in our stomachs. Has He let us go hungry?"

He was quiet for a moment, so she nudged him.

"A little," he said contritely.

Poor Burl. He was a growing boy with an increasing appetite. "A little hungry isn't so bad."

"I guess not."

"You go back to bed and get some sleep."

He stood. "What about you? You need sleep, too."

He worried about her more than she realized. "I'm almost through here. I'll put out the light soon."

Burl padded out in stocking feet. She noticed a hole in the bottom of one of his socks and sighed. She couldn't keep up with all this family needed. *Lord, deliver us.* Setting her mending aside, she blew out the candle then crawled into bed with a shiver, curling around Miles's warm body.

seven

Ian strode up to his shop, his key ready for the lock, and froze. Someone had smashed the door glass, and the broken pieces were strewn about on the floor inside. He opened the door and crunched on the shards. Somewhere in the back, Fred yapped incessantly. "Conner?"

"Back here," Conner called.

He headed toward Conner's voice. "What happened to the front door?"

"We got rid of one rat and caught another." Conner pointed to the edge of his bed.

He couldn't believe it. "Burl? You did that?" He thumbed back toward the front of the shop.

Burl's lower lip quivered, and tears rolled down his cheeks. "I didn't know no one was here."

"What were you doing? Why did you break my front window?"

Burl pursed his lips and lowered his head.

Ian hunkered down in front of him so he could see the boy's face. "Why, Burl? I thought you liked me."

"I like you," Burl mumbled.

"Then why?"

Burl's lips tightened.

Conner took a step toward the door. "I'll sweep up the broken glass before we have any customers."

He stood. "No. Burl will clean up the mess."

Burl looked up at him with wide blue eyes. Eyes like his sister's.

"Mr. Jackson will show you where the broom and dust-pan are."

Conner scooped up Fred. "This way."

Burl scooted off the bed and followed.

Ian went out to the front to assess any further damage. It appeared that the door window was the only casualty.

Burl shuffled by, dragging the broom behind him, and then started sweeping glass to the dustpan that kept scooting away by the broom's movement. Burl tried this method for only a moment more before he put his foot on the dustpan, but this tipped the front up just enough for the shards to go under it. He stopped and stared at the broom, then the dustpan, then the glass.

Ian could see that Burl was trying to figure out just how to accomplish the task. He would give the boy direction if he asked for it.

Burl didn't look to him. He just stared at his problem then leaned the broom against the wall, took the dustpan in hand, and pushed the shards toward the wall and scooped them up into the dust pan. He then turned and looked at Ian.

Ian pointed to the waste bucket Conner had brought out.

Burl dumped most of the glass into it with only a few pieces falling back to the floor.

Conner leaned toward Ian. "Should we tell him there's an easier way?"

"It's interesting to watch him puzzle out the problem and come up with his own solutions. He's quite an intelligent boy."

Burl worked diligently for ten minutes, having gotten most of the glass. He pushed some of the finer pieces up against the wall and wiggled the dustpan to get them into it. He reached his finger down toward the glass slivers as if to push them into the pan.

"Don't use your hand. You'll cut yourself." Ian came around the counter.

Burl looked up at him. "I can't get any more."

He showed the boy how to sweep the remaining glass into a pile and, with the broom resting on his shoulder against his neck, showed him how to sweep the pile into the dustpan. Burl took to this method and finished the process. He took the broom and dustpan back to the closet Conner had shown him. "What time is it?"

Ian pulled out his pocket watch. "Nine o'clock. Just in time for opening."

"I'm 'posed to be in school." The boy headed for the door.

"Not so fast."

"But I have to. Alice will be mad if I miss school."

"Who is going to pay for a new window?"

Burl looked from him to the window then down to the floor. "Me, sir?"

"That would be the right thing to do."

"But I ain't got no money."

"I *don't have any* money."

Burl took a deep breath. "I don't have any money."

"Well then, you'll need a job."

"Alice don't want me to get no job. She wants me to get schoolin'. But I can get a job and pay for the window and Alice don't have to know I'm not in school. I don't learn nothin' at school anyway. Mr. Kray don't know nothin'."

The boy could use a few more grammar lessons. "Mr. Kray *doesn't know anything*."

Burl scrunched up his face. "Mr. Kray doesn't know anything."

"Did you break my window so you wouldn't have to go to school?"

Burl looked down. "No, sir."

"Why did you break my window then?" He wanted to get an answer to his question.

Burl scuffed his worn brogan on the floor but didn't say anything.

Ian waited. "Well?"

"Can I go now?"

"I'll walk you to school and explain to Mr. Kray why you are late."

Burl's eyes widened like saucers. "Oh no, sir. Please don't do that."

"Conner, I'll be back as soon as I can, and I'll stop by the glazier on my way back and see when this window can be replaced."

Conner nodded. "I'll see if I can find something to cover it with until then."

As Ian walked Burl to school, the boy asked, "Are you gonna tell Alice about this?"

"No, son." He paused as Burl let out a sigh. "You are."

Burl jerked his head up. "Me? I ain't tellin' her nothin'."

"Yes, you will." He would be there to make sure of it.

Burl folded his arms across his chest.

When they got to the schoolhouse and entered the classroom, Ian said, "Mr. Kray, it's my fault Burl Martin is late this morning. I had him doing a few chores around my store."

Mr. Kray stood from his desk chair. "And here I was looking forward to a quiet day." He turned to Burl with narrowing eyes. "The arithmetic examination is half over. You'd better get a move on if you want to answer even one question. Don't think I'll give you any extra time."

Burl scurried to his seat.

Ian had met Mr. Kray before and hadn't been impressed with the man. "Mr. Kray, it's my fault he's late. The boy shouldn't be punished for it."

"I'll run my classroom as I see fit, and you are a disruption."

If Burl was right and Mr. Kray "don't know nothin'," he also didn't have any manners. He'd had teachers like Mr. Kray who were intimidated by his intelligence. "Burl, I'll be back for you when school lets out."

Burl rolled his eyes and wilted onto the desk.

❧

Ian stood by the bare oak tree in the schoolyard until Burl came out of the building. Two older boys cajoled him. They seemed to be trying to goad him into something. Probably the same two boys who had helped him into trouble on the ship last week. And maybe talked him into breaking into the pharmacy.

When Burl saw Ian, he sobered and walked away from the other two. "I didn't think you'd really come."

"We have to talk to your sister about this morning."

Burl's eyes puckered. "Please don't. She worries too much. I'll do anythin' you want; just please don't tell her."

He felt sorry for the boy and wanted to give him the grace of a pardon, but he was doing that in not taking this matter to the police as he could. He had a plan. "We *are* going to your apartment right now, and you *are* going to tell her what you did."

"She won't be there. She's out lookin' for a job, so you don't have to waste your time." The boy shoved his hands into his pockets and started walking away as if the matter were settled.

He caught up to him. "I'll wait."

Burl stopped and stared at him. "You'll give Grandpa a heart attack."

"I doubt that."

"You really gonna make me do this?"

"Yes." He hoped it wouldn't be as bad as Burl was trying to lead him to believe, and he hoped he was doing the right thing. They walked along in silence except for the sound of Burl's shuffling feet. "How did you fare on the arithmetic examination?"

"I finished it."

"Did Mr. Kray give you extra time after all?"

"Nah. I finished in time. It was baby work."

"So you did well despite the shorter time?" Good for the boy.

Burl blasted a huge smile. "I got them all right. Mr. Kray was fumin' mad at that."

No wonder the boy hated school. Not only did he have a bad teacher, but he was bored. Ian understood all too well the feeling of being bored in school, but he'd had some good teachers along the way. Miss Hanson had been his favorite.

She was pretty, but she also brought in stacks of books for him. He'd been required to take the same examinations that the other students would be taking. If he passed them, he could learn whatever he wanted on his own while she taught the class. Burl needed someone to challenge his mind.

"Who were those two boys you were with?"

Burl picked up a long stick. "Just boys."

"Are they your friends?"

The stick hissed as it dragged on the ground behind the boy. "Sure."

Ian would guess they weren't the kind of friends that were good for him. "Do you do a lot of things with them?"

Burl shrugged. "I guess."

"Were they with you that day on the ship?"

Burl looked up at him with big, round blue eyes, evidently surprised he'd guessed.

"And did they talk you into breaking into my store?"

Burl suddenly became fascinated with the mud beneath his feet. The boy didn't have to reply; Ian had gotten his answer. "Those two are quite a bit older than you, aren't they?"

The boy nodded slightly.

He'd guess maybe eighth grade. "They aren't very good friends to keep getting you in trouble."

Burl kept his focus down and his mouth shut.

"The friends you choose can guide your life. They can take you in a good direction. . .or a bad one."

Burl raised his gaze to him. "What if they choose you?"

"You can say no."

"They're bigger than me, both of them."

The poor boy felt trapped. Ian would have to think of some way to help him break free of those two troublemaking ruffians.

❧

Alice trudged up the steps toward the apartment. She leaned against the wall next to the door. *Lord, give me strength to face my family still without any prospects of a job.*

The door opened, and Grandpa stepped into the hall. When he saw her, he closed the door behind him.

Tears pooled in her eyes. "I'm out of places to look. I guess I'll have to go up to the sawmill and see if they'll hire me as a cook. If they do, we'll have to move closer."

"The Lord will provide."

She held up a sack. "Minister Pepper gave me some more food. At least we can eat tonight. I don't know how much more he can afford to give away."

"Well, come inside. There's someone here to see you."

She squared her shoulders and followed Grandpa inside. Mr. MacGregor stood beside a chair that Burl sat in. Burl looked pale. She ran and knelt in front of him. "Are you sick?" She finger combed his bangs off his forehead. "Are you all right?"

Burl pulled away from her hand.

She stood and looked at Mr. MacGregor.

"Mrs. Dempsey, it's a pleasure to see you again. I wish it were under better circumstances."

A sickening feeling twisted her stomach. *Lord, give me strength.* "What's wrong?"

Mr. MacGregor put a hand on Burl's shoulder. "Burl, tell your sister."

She turned her gaze on her brother. "What have you done this time?"

"I broke Mr. MacGregor's window. It was an accident, honest."

"Like throwing the barrels over the side of the ship was an accident? Oh Burl, when will you ever learn?"

"Sebastian and Murphy said we could sell some of the stuff and get money; then I could buy food so you wouldn't have to work so hard."

Where had she gone wrong if Burl thought stealing was the way to solve their problems? "Burl, stealing won't make it better."

She mustered her courage and turned back to Mr. MacGregor. She hoped he would be understanding. "Are you going to notify the police?"

"Not if a couple of conditions are met."

"I'll pay for the window." When she got a job.

"That won't be necessary. Burl will come to work for me before school and after school until it's paid off."

He wasn't going to notify the police. She gave a sigh of relief. He was a nice man. "That's very generous of you."

"I can go with him to make sure he does as he is told," Grandpa said.

"That won't be necessary, Mr. Greig. Burl will do as he's told. Won't you, boy?"

"Yes, sir."

"I do have one other condition. You come to work for me, too."

She jerked her gaze to his face. "What?"

"I could use another assistant at the store."

He was going to use her poor circumstance against her. "I'm afraid that won't be possible."

"Did you secure other employment?"

"No, but. . ." She didn't want him using this to take advantage of the situation. She wanted him to stay a nice man.

"Then you'll come work for me. I insist."

She looked from him to Burl to Grandpa. Tears welled, and she strode to her room. Latching the door, she leaned against it. *Dear Lord, what do I do? Is Mr. MacGregor using my poor circumstances and Burl's bad behavior to take advantage? Please let him just be a nice man with no ulterior motives.*

An alliance with Mr. MacGregor was tenuous at best. She was afraid. Afraid of him. Afraid of what he might do. . .to her heart. She couldn't trust herself where men were concerned. She had poor judgment. Very poor judgment.

⁂

"Mama cry," Miles popped his thumb into his mouth and

wrapped his free arm around Arthur's leg.

Ian raked a hand through his hair. "I shouldn't have pushed."

"Do you really have a position available?" Arthur asked.

"There are tasks that Conner and I aren't able to get to. Another pair of hands would be helpful."

Arthur nodded. "Then stand your ground."

"I thought she would be happy. I've only served to anger her." He ached for her suffering. He ached to help her. He ached that she'd shut him out.

Burl tugged on his sleeve. "Did you mean it? Me workin' for you?"

"Of course. You have a window to pay for."

The boy's mouth spread into a wide grin. "Even after I got the window paid for, can I still work for you?"

"We'll see how you do first. If you're not a hard worker, I can't rightly keep you on."

"Oh, I'll work hard, I promise. Real hard."

He hoped the boy did. "You can't bring your friends around."

"I won't. I promise."

Lots of promises. He hoped the boy could keep them.

eight

The next morning as Ian approached his shop, he saw Burl out front with a broom. "You're working already."

"Yes, sir. I'm a hard worker." Burl didn't break his stride. The boy apparently intended to prove just how hard a worker he was.

"Is your sister coming today?"

"Don't know. She's in a sour mood this mornin'. It's best not to talk to her when she's like that."

He would have to remember that. "Make sure you get the corners in the doorway."

"I will. Mr. Jackson showed me just what to do. Said iffin I don't do it right, I'll be doin' it again." Burl held the door open for him.

Ian went inside and found Conner near the window, looking out. "I see you put him to work already."

"He said he was here to work. I thought out front might be the safest place to start until we had two sets of eyes to watch over him."

He smiled. "Thank you for having him sweep out there. I guess I've neglected the sidewalk."

Conner leaned on the counter. "Since a certain beautiful lady no longer works next door, you've been spending less time out there."

"You're a perceptive fellow."

Conner gave him a crooked smile. "The glazier will come this morning to replace the broken window."

"With any luck, Mrs. Dempsey will come in to work today."

"I thought that was one of your conditions for not handing

73

her brother over to the police."

"It was, but she wasn't happy with the idea."

"Why?"

"I have no idea, except that Arthur said she didn't like to be beholden to any man. I just want to help her and her family. She needs work, and I can provide that for her. 'Bear ye one another's burdens' and all that." Ian paused. "I'm glad she let Burl come."

"I sure hope you still feel that way at the end of the day."

"Burl will keep his word." He had to believe that.

❧

Alice stopped just short of the pharmacy. *Lord, thank You for this job. Please let it be a genuine job and not a concocted scheme for a man to use me again.* She took a deep breath then entered the store. She stared around at shelf after shelf after shelf of medicines lining both walls of the long, narrow room. Medicines were in the glass display counters, too. There were too many. She'd never be able to learn this all.

Mr. MacGregor smiled at her and came over. "Good morning."

"Good morning." She removed her hat. "I wasn't sure just when you wanted me here. I hope I'm not late or haven't caused you any inconvenience."

"You have caused no inconvenience." He held out his hand. "Let me put away your coat and hat." After taking them to the back, he returned.

She shook her head. "I can't do this. It's too much."

"Like I said, you won't be working directly with the medicines. Along this wall are the pharmacy medicines; the other wall has the folk remedies."

"You have both?"

"Some of the pharmaceuticals started out as home remedies. And there's a reason some of these remedies have been used for generations. They work."

This would be no simple job for her. There wouldn't be

any sewing or mending. She stood next to her brother. "Burl, you're going to be late for school."

Burl straightened up from his task of sorting small corked bottles and untied his apron.

"Burl, don't leave just yet. I need to talk to your sister first," Mr. MacGregor said.

Her brother pulled his eyebrows together and looked from Mr. MacGregor to her.

Mr. MacGregor turned to her. "May I speak with you in the back for a minute?"

She followed him. "I don't want him to be late for school. I have enough trouble getting him to behave."

"I know. I'll get right to the point. I want him to stay here at the store."

"All day?"

He nodded.

She put her hands on her hips. "I want him to get schooling so he doesn't have to work at the mill or in a factory. That's no kind of life. I don't want him missing an arm like Grandpa." Grandpa never complained, but the horror was still fresh in her mind.

"I'll teach him."

She knit her brows together. What was he up to? "You?"

"I was at the school yesterday after he broke in here. The teacher was condescending to him and wouldn't extend the time for him to take the arithmetic examination that the other students had already half finished."

"Maybe he'll learn to behave and not be late."

"It only served to prove to him that he didn't need to be on time. He finished the examination on time and got all the questions right."

Her brother was very smart. She knew it, and Grandpa knew it, but the rest of the world needed the proof of his finishing school. Why did Mr. MacGregor even care? "My brother may be smart, but he hasn't learned everything he needs to know yet."

"I can teach him far more than he'll learn at the school."

Was he scheming with Burl? She narrowed her eyes. "Did Burl put you up to this?"

He shook his head. "This was my own idea."

Anger boiled inside. He was going to use Burl to get to her. "I get it, and I don't like this one bit."

"Why not? It's a good solution."

"You're trying to turn my brother against me." She didn't think it would take much. He was already severely discontent with school and with her. With a lot of things.

"What? No. I just want to help."

"You and he have this all worked out, and if I go back out there and tell Burl he still has to go to the school, I'll look like a mean, unreasonable sister. He'll side with you, and the only way I will get any peace will be to give in."

"You have it all wrong. Burl knows nothing of this. It is your decision, not his. I would never speak to him about this before you."

"He really doesn't know anything about this matter?"

"No."

Her anger cooled. "I still want him to get formal schooling."

"He will. I made arrangements with the headmaster to teach him here, and he will go into the school every week and take the examinations that all the other students take."

Her anger rose again. "You talked to the school without my consent?"

"No. I. . .I. . ."

She didn't like other people meddling in her life.

"The headmaster came into the store yesterday after I took Burl home. I spoke to him then. I only want to help. Burl runs around with two older boys who are responsible for getting him in trouble down at the docks last week. I saw those boys trying to talk him into something else. I believe they are Sebastian and Murphy, the ones who talked him into breaking in here. If he does his schooling here, he won't be around those boys and hopefully won't get into trouble."

He had a point, but she hated being more in debt to this man, to any man. Was he arranging things to take advantage of his position? She nodded. "Okay."

He smiled at her, and her heart danced.

"Do you want to tell him?"

She shook her head. "You can, but he'd better not fall behind."

"He won't. His teacher will have a hard time keeping up with his exams." Mr. MacGregor went out to the front.

What was she getting herself into?

She heard Burl's excited voice; then he met her as she came out of the back. "Is it true? Is Mr. MacGregor really gonna teach me?"

Burl really hadn't known. It warmed her heart. "Yes. But you have to study hard and do as you're told. And no mischief."

"I will." Burl had a huge grin when he turned away.

Mr. MacGregor smiled at her again. "He'll be better off. You'll see. You'll all be better off."

So it seemed. She nodded. A bit of hope replaced a small piece of the constant struggle to survive that hounded her. But she knew she couldn't count on this to last.

☙

Ian re-added the column of numbers. He'd just recorded the amount he was paying for his telephone bill here at the store. He'd already added it four times and gotten four different answers. He should just get it over with. No matter how he worded it, she would take it wrong and be mad at him. She was nearby cleaning a shelf.

"Mrs. Dempsey, I have a request to make of you."

She squared her shoulders and folded her arms across the front of her work apron. "What is it?"

He took a deep breath. "I'd like to buy you a skirt and blouse."

She narrowed her eyes.

So he quickly added, "For work." Then he looked across the store. "Conner, can you come here a minute?"

Conner left what he was doing with Burl and came over. "What can I do for you?"

"Who bought your suit?"

"You did."

"Why?"

"I didn't have a suit to wear to work."

He turned back to Alice. "I'd like to do the same for you. Not that you don't look nice, but I'd like you to be in a navy or black skirt with a white blouse."

She looked down at her faded yellow print dress. "I'll make them myself, as soon as I have the money to purchase the yard goods."

He shook his head. "Because I'm requiring it for work, I'll buy them. I'd like to go out today and buy them so you have them as soon as possible."

She narrowed her eyes sharply at him. "May I speak with you privately in the back?"

Conner raised his eyebrows. "I'll go check on Burl."

Ian followed Alice to the back.

"Mr. MacGregor, I don't think it is appropriate for you to buy me clothes."

"It is only from a business standpoint. Customers have more confidence in my knowledge and my store when I and my employees dress professionally."

"I guess that would be acceptable."

"I would also like to buy something for Burl as he will be spending a lot of time here at the store." He wished he had an excuse to buy Arthur and Miles new clothes as well.

She gave a small nod of defeat.

That hadn't gone as badly as he'd anticipated.

"Mr. MacGregor, I need to know what the terms of my employment are here with you. The exact terms."

Ian nodded. "You are an employee in my store."

"For how long? Just until my brother repays his debt to you? Is my pay going toward the window as well?"

"Burl is responsible for paying for the whole window. You will be paid a fair wage for your work."

"Anything else?"

"Like what?"

"Do you have any other expectations where I am concerned?"

He suddenly felt ill at ease and pulled at his bat's-wing tie. "I don't know what you're getting at."

"Let's not play games here. I am a young woman in need—we both know that—and you are a man of some means. Are you expecting anything more than simply having me work in your store?"

Ian felt his face flush. "Mrs. Dempsey, I would never suggest anything inappropriate. You are my employee, nothing more."

She nodded and returned to the front.

He slumped into a nearby chair. That did it for him. He couldn't very well try to court her now that he'd insisted she was only an employee to him. She would never be only an employee to him. *Lord in heaven, change her heart toward me. Show me how to proceed.* He paused.

"*Patience.*"

I'm to have patience with her? Then that was what he'd do.

Mr. MacGregor returned from the back. "At which dress shop do you usually purchase your clothing?"

"Usually?" Why must everything he asked emphasize her lack of means? Wasn't there one thing about her that could impress him? She shook off that thought. She was not here to catch his eye. "I have never had the good fortune to buy store clothes."

"You make all your clothes?"

She nodded, not sure if he was impressed by that or repulsed.

"Burl's, too? And the rest of your family?"

"There is nothing wrong with making one's clothing."

"I'm not saying that. It's just that often you can tell when people in the city are wearing homespun clothing. Yours look like store-bought clothes. You must be an excellent seamstress."

"Oh." She tried not to smile and get puffed up with pride, but she couldn't help but feel good about her God-given talent. And Mr. MacGregor's compliment.

"If you have no preference, on the next block is Cameo's. We'll go there."

"Not there."

Mr. MacGregor raised his eyebrows. "Is there a reason? My tailor is next door and owns both stores. I can have Burl fitted while you are at Cameo's."

How could she tell him she'd been fired from there nearly a year ago when Burl had been cutting shines and she'd had to miss work too often. "Cameo's is fine. I'll go get my things." She looked at the oversized, ill-fitting man's coat from decades ago that Sally and Marjorie had given her. She couldn't go into Cameo's wearing that. She swung her shawl around her shoulders and pinned on her hat. Her shawl wouldn't be nearly warm enough, but Cameo's was only a short distance away.

It was quite cold above ground, and she almost regretted not wearing the old coat by the time they reached Cameo's, but once she saw the look of disdain on Charlotte's face, she regretted coming at all.

Charlotte strode over with purpose. "Alice, you know I don't have any work for you."

"Mrs. Freeman, I'm Ian MacGregor. I have employed Mrs. Dempsey and require different attire for work. Please find her a white blouse and dark skirt, and anything else she needs. I will be next door having the boy fitted as he is working in my store as well."

Charlotte gave a simple nod. "I'll take care of it."

After the door closed behind Mr. MacGregor and Burl, Charlotte turned to her. "So you cast your net and caught yourself a man."

"I did no such thing."

"There's no shame in it. With your looks, you should be looking for a man and not a job. A catch like Mr. MacGregor is no small thing."

"I am not out to catch Mr. MacGregor or anyone else for a husband." Why did everyone think she needed a husband?

"Pity." Charlotte started walking. "Come this way." She stopped and pulled five white shirtwaists off the rack and draped them over her arm. "I believe these are your size."

Charlotte was going to wait on her and not pass her off to one of the other girls? She must be trying to impress Mr. MacGregor.

At another rack, Charlotte said, "What color of skirt do you prefer? Black? Navy? I have a nice deep green."

Mr. MacGregor had said navy or black. "Navy, please."

Charlotte pulled three long skirts and headed for a dressing room. "Let me know if you require anything else or if you need a different size."

She nodded. "Thank you."

"You would be wise to set your cap for Mr. MacGregor." Charlotte drew the curtain across the opening of the dressing room.

She sighed. She was not setting her cap for that man. She put on a shirtwaist with tucks at the shoulders and pleats in the back. How many of these had she sewn while working here? She pulled on a skirt that she could have made. She wished Mr. MacGregor hadn't insisted on buying store clothes. She could easily make these for less money.

"Alice?"

She pulled back the curtain.

Charlotte held out a strip of cloth. "Yes, this matches the

skirt." She tied it in a bow around Alice's neck then smiled. "Lovely."

Alice turned to the mirror. She looked like a Gibson girl featured in *Harper's Bazaar*. She didn't feel worthless in these clothes. It was amazing how nicer clothes could make you feel better about yourself.

Charlotte looked over her shoulder into the mirror. "I think Mr. MacGregor will be pleased."

That made her insides tickle, but she was not out to please Mr. MacGregor with her looks or clothing. Besides, Mr. MacGregor didn't judge people's value by how they looked— at least, she hoped not.

She went next door and found the pair sitting. Mr. MacGregor stood when she entered, and smiled. "You look lovely."

A smile rose up in her that he was pleased. "If it can wait a few days, I could sew these for much less money."

"Nonsense."

Burl stood. "I'm gettin' a suit."

Mr. MacGregor's gaze stayed firmly attached to her. "We're waiting for the alterations. They should be completed soon."

A suit? "Burl isn't old enough for a full suit. It's too much. A simple shirt and pants will suffice."

Sadness flittered in Mr. MacGregor's eyes. "The suit will also suffice."

She wished she hadn't sounded like she was scolding him. She much preferred his pleasure to his disappointment.

❧

At the end of the workday, Alice came up to Ian. "Mr. MacGregor, I have a small request."

He was surprised to see her back in her yellow dress, then glanced at Burl in his old clothes, holding Fred. "You didn't have to change out of your work clothes."

"They would get ruined in the muddy streets."

He nodded. Practical woman. "What is your request?"

"As you have no doubt noticed, we don't have a lot. I was

wondering if you could spare my day's wage."

He studied her a moment. Were they really that close to starving? He opened the cash register and handed her the wages for the day. He would note it in his accounting book later. It must have been hard for her to come and ask. "I was very pleased with your work today." He turned to Burl and ruffled his hair. "And yours, too." He walked them to the door.

"Good-bye, Fred." Burl nuzzled his face into the dog's scruffy fur before setting her down.

"I'll see you both tomorrow." Ian shut and locked the door behind them then watched them walk to the corner.

Conner came up beside him. "I hope you know what you're doing."

"Me, too." It just felt right to have them both there. *Lord, help me guide and direct Burl on the right path. A path that leads to Your will for his life.*

Conner put a hand on his shoulder. "I'm just glad it's you this time instead of me."

"Me what?"

"Being the hero."

"I'm no hero."

"You are to her," Conner said.

"I doubt that. She looks at me with suspicion."

"You've given her a job so she can feed her family, you've rescued her brother from getting into further trouble, and you're giving him a better education than he can get at the public school. I think that qualifies you as her hero."

Conner was some kind of character. "I don't think she's looking for a hero."

"I think she likes you."

He shook his head. "Conner, you ever think about writing dime novels? Because you have quite an imagination."

Conner just smiled.

Ian had to smile, too. Anything he could do to gain Alice's

trust—and maybe one day her heart—was good.

❧

Alice headed straight for the grocers. She gathered up enough food for three days. When was the last time she'd been able to buy food for that many days? *Thank You, Lord.* She looked at what she had and calculated how much it would cost, then added a skein of red no. 8 spun truck to her lot. She had some knitting to do. After paying, she hurried home.

"I was beginning to worry." Grandpa stood from where he sat at the table.

"Don't get up." She hurried over to the table and helped him back into the chair.

Burl set the bulging old flour sack he carried onto the table. "We got food for three whole days, and Mr. MacGregor buyed me a suit."

"*Bought* you a suit." Her correction didn't dampen his good mood.

"Bought. And he teached—I mean taught me all sorts of things."

Grandpa nodded. "Go wash up so you can help your sister with supper."

"But—"

Grandpa gave him his "don't argue with me" look, and Burl scampered off.

"How did work go?"

She didn't want to think about it. "Terrible."

Grandpa raised his eyebrows. "That bad?"

"Oh, I'm not fired. At least not yet. I probably should be but not for anything Burl did. He worked really hard. You would've been proud of him. Mr. MacGregor is going to school him."

"He is? Was that his idea?"

She nodded.

"I'll guess that sits well with the lad."

Sit well? Burl looked up at Mr. MacGregor like Fred

looked at Mr. Jackson when he had food for the dog. "Burl did everything Mr. MacGregor told him to do. He behaved perfectly. I wonder how long that will last."

"This might be just what the boy needs, a father figure in his life. So what did you do that was so bad?"

She sighed. "I insulted Mr. MacGregor. I implied he was less than honorable. His face turned red." Her heart had stirred at his embarrassment, and she wished she could recapture her careless accusation. "I don't want to go back."

"But you must."

nine

When Alice came in the next day, Burl was already sitting at the far end of the counter with a book open in front of him. Mr. MacGregor was sorting money into the cash register. Fred did not come to greet her, an indication of Mr. Jackson's absence. "Where's Mr. Jackson?"

"He's at the dock. He has a friend from his childhood who is a captain, so even when I'm not expecting a shipment, he likes to go down there."

"The same captain of the ship that Burl. . .was on?"

He gave a nod. "The same."

That had been one of her more terrifying days. "I really appreciate Mr. Jackson's helping Burl out that day."

Mr. MacGregor's eyes narrowed slightly.

She wondered why but let it pass as she took a deep breath. "You said that it was Mr. Jackson's idea to have the reading material in the store, and he suggested selling some of your garden vegetables when they're in season."

"That's right. Conner has a keen eye for business. He will do well when he opens his own store."

She pulled out a three-foot-long knitted scarf. "I was wondering if I could put out scarves I knit. In all this damp, cold weather, a scarf will help keep people's necks warm and help them not to get so many sore throats and colds."

"Then they wouldn't need my medicines."

She looked down. "I didn't think of that." She was hoping to make some extra money.

"I like it. Preventative treatment. I would rather help keep my customers healthy than try to get them well after they are sick." He held out his hand.

She handed him the scarf.

He wrapped it around his neck then wiggled his fingers through the three-inch slit she'd knitted into it. "There's a hole in it."

"It's to tuck the other end in to keep it tight. That way you don't have to have a big knot under your chin."

He raised an eyebrow.

She stepped up to him and tucked the end through the slit. "Like that." She looked up into his down-turned face, and her pulse quickened.

"Thank you," he whispered then cleared his throat. " 'The pharmacy that keeps you well so you don't need our medicine.' I'll take it." He pulled out his wallet and paid her.

"You?"

"It wouldn't do my customers any good for me to be sick. How would I help them? How many more do you have?"

"That's the only one. I can go at lunch, if you'll let me, and get more spun truck. I can knit at lunch and when we aren't busy and you have no other chores for me, if that would be all right with you."

"Of course. The store will get a small percentage of the price from the scarves, but the rest will be yours."

"Yes. I knew that was the way you worked it with Mr. Jackson and the reading material." Her hopes soared. She'd be making a little extra money. She'd buy the boys new shoes and fabric scraps to make a new quilt for Grandpa and Burl's bed. Then maybe a new dress for herself. And of course enough food for everyone to eat their fill.

❧

A week later when Alice arrived at the store, she strolled to the back and into the storage room where her work clothes hung. *Work clothes*, she mused. They were the nicest clothes she had. As she hung up her worn, faded dress, she noticed Burl's nice work clothes still on the peg. What was Mr. MacGregor having him do that he'd still be in his old clothes?

She tied an apron around her waist and took a bucket of water and a rag out to the front. She didn't see her brother anywhere. "Where's Burl?" He always arrived ahead of her even if they left home at the same time.

Conner raised his head. "Not in yet."

Panic tightened her chest. "He should've been here well before me."

Mr. MacGregor came around the counter to her. "We haven't seen him this morning."

Just then Burl scurried through the front door, his jacket askew and dirt on his face. With his head ducked, he hurried for the back room.

She stepped into his path. "I was worried about you." She took in the tear in his jacket where the sleeve was separated from the shoulder. "What happened?"

Burl shot a look to Mr. MacGregor. "Nothin'."

"You didn't leave home like this."

He shrugged and darted around her.

She turned to Mr. MacGregor and put her hands on her hips. "What do you know?"

"I don't know anything."

"But Burl gave you a knowing look. Like the two of you have a secret."

"No secret. I just suspect he might have been taking care of some old business. Growing into trying to be a man."

Old business? Trying to be a man? What "old business" could he possibly have? She wasn't ready for him to be a man yet.

❧

A week later, as Ian turned the corner and strode toward his store, two youths ran along the sidewalk away from him. What were they doing down here this early? Then he saw his store windows smashed, all of them.

He could hear Fred whining from somewhere within. "Conner?" He wrenched open the door and crunched on broken glass. "Conner!" He headed toward the sound of whimpering.

Conner lay motionless behind one of the counters. Fred sat next to him, whining as she licked a cut on Conner's forehead.

He quickly went to his knees beside his friend, checking for a pulse on his neck and looking to see if he was breathing. Conner's chest rose and fell in short, rapid succession, and his heart drummed out a strong beat beneath his fingers. "Conner, can you hear me?"

Conner moaned but didn't open his eyes.

"Hold on. I'll be right back." He ran to his telephone and rang for the hospital. He'd wondered about the wisdom of spending the money on the telephone when he rarely used it. His customers didn't have telephones in their homes to call him. He didn't even have a telephone in his home. Few people did. Now he was very glad he'd spent the money and paid the monthly fee.

"First Providence Hospital."

He spoke into the mouthpiece. "I have an injured man. Send a doctor." He gave the address and hung up.

He rushed back to Conner's side. "Help will be here soon. Can you speak to me?"

Conner moved his head slightly and winced but made no sound. Other than the cut on the man's forehead, Ian couldn't see any other injuries.

≥♦

The doctor arrived down the back stairs with Mr. Lansky, Ian's landlord, who ran his own store upstairs at street level. Ian showed the doctor to Conner and told them both what happened.

Mr. Lansky noticed the broken glass. "I'll notify the police, as well."

"Thank you."

Burl came through the front door then. "Mr. MacGregor, what happened?"

"Someone broke in and hurt Conner. Now stay back."

"Mr. Jackson's hurt?" Burl's voice cracked.

The doctor examined Conner. When he moved Conner's arm, Conner moaned and held his breath. The doctor unbuttoned Conner's cuff and gently pulled up his sleeve. The arm was red and swollen.

Ian guessed it was broken.

The doctor looked up to him. "I'm going to need two sticks to splint this with."

Silent tears rolled down Burl's face.

Ian grabbed the boy by the arm and hustled him to the back. "Find me a board or two sticks, twelve to eighteen inches long."

"Is Mr. Jackson gonna die?"

He hoped not. Conner had moaned a couple of times and felt pain. Those were both good signs. "I don't think so. Now find me that wood." He needed to get the boy's mind off of Conner.

A police officer came down the back stairs then. "I hear you had a bit of trouble."

He gave his full attention to the officer as Burl went off hunting for a splint. "Someone broke in and injured one of my employees."

"Did you see who it was?"

"Whoever it was left before I got here. I did see two boys running along the sidewalk when I came up, but there's no way to know if it was them."

Burl gasped. He was standing with two slim boards in his hands.

"Take those to the doctor straightaway."

Burl ran to the other room.

"Can you identify the boys?" the officer asked.

Ian shook his head. "They had their backs to me." He'd have looked at their size and build a bit more closely if he'd known they might have broken into his store or anyone else's.

"Is anything missing?"

"I haven't had a chance to look." It would take him a while to figure that out with the mess to clean up.

"Burl?" he heard Alice exclaim in a panicked voice.

"Alice," Burl replied.

"Excuse me, Officer." He hurried out to Alice, whose face was pale. Burl was at her side crying. Although Burl was nearly as tall as Alice, he was still just a boy.

"What happened?" Alice asked.

"Mr. Jackson's hurt. Bad," Burl forced out in a strained voice.

Alice's eyes widened. "Is he—"

"I think he'll be fine. The doctor is looking at him."

The officer approached them. "What can the two of you tell me about this?"

"I just arrived." Alice shook her head.

He imagined she was trying to understand just what had happened herself. It was a lot to take in all at once. He wanted to hold her and comfort her but he didn't. "They arrived after me."

"When you have a chance, look around and let me know if anything is missing."

"Officer"—the doctor poked his head up from behind the counter—"can you go upstairs and see if the ambulance is here and send down the stretcher?" The officer left.

"I tried to stop 'em," Burl whined.

"Stop who?" Ian directed his gaze at Burl's worried face.

"Murphy and Sebastian."

"Are those the two boys who got you in trouble before?"

Burl nodded.

It made some sense. If he thought about the two boys he'd seen Burl with two weeks ago at the school and the two running along the sidewalk, they could be the same ones. "Why do you think Murphy and Sebastian had something to do with this?"

"They comed to me last week."

He wouldn't worry about correcting the boy's grammar. "Do tell."

"They were mad because I didn't bring them nothin' when I broke in, and then I didn't come back to school."

"That was the day you came later than usual and your coat was torn."

Burl sniffled. "Yes, sir."

He was glad Burl was away from those two boys for the most part. "What did they ask you to do?"

"They wanted to know where this place was so they could come steal your medicines themselves. But I didn't tell them. I told 'em that you had a man guardin' it all the time, and there was a big mean dog that would tear them up."

He doubted Fred would hurt the boys. They weren't the sort of rat Conner was training her to go after. Poor Burl didn't realize he'd given the boys exactly what they needed to come prepared.

"How'd they find your store? I didn't tell them. Honest."

"I know you didn't. They probably followed you."

Burl paled.

"It wasn't your fault. You had no way to know what they'd do."

Burl nodded weakly. "Where's Fred?"

Ian glanced around. "She was here when I arrived."

"Did they hurt her, too?"

"No, she was fine." She'd probably cowered in the corner, scared to death, the poor thing.

"Fred," Burl began calling through his tears.

"Why don't you look in the back and in Mr. Jackson's room for her?" It would be good for the boy to stay busy with something useful.

Burl trotted off toward the back, calling for Fred.

"I'm going to find the officer and have him talk to Burl."

Alice looked a bit shaken. She nodded. "I'll see if the doctor needs any help."

"Thank you." He took the stairs two at a time.

The officer stood near the front door with Mr. Lansky. "So you didn't hear anything?"

Mr. Lansky shook his head. "I didn't know anything was amiss downstairs until the doctor arrived."

"So the only witness can't tell me anything at the moment. I guess I can't do much until the poor bloke wakes up."

Ian stopped next to the men. "I may be able to help."

The officer turned to him. "I thought you didn't see anything."

"I have learned of some additional information."

The officer's face brightened. "The sooner I can hunt down a lead, the better chance I have of catching who is responsible."

"The boy downstairs knows a couple of boys who were asking him about my store. Since Burl wouldn't break in for them, they told him that they would do it themselves."

The officer turned to Mr. Lansky, but before he could say anything, Mr. Lansky said, "I'll send down the stretcher when it gets here."

Ian led the officer downstairs and into Conner's private room, where Burl lay on the floor, the top half of his body hidden under the bed.

"Burl, can you come out of there?"

"Fred's not under here," Burl said as he wiggled out from under the bed. He stood and wiped the tears from his cheeks when he saw the officer.

"Fred is Mr. Jackson's dog," Ian explained.

The officer nodded then turned to Burl. "I hear you might know something about who broke in and hurt Mr. Jackson."

Burl looked to Ian.

He put a reassuring hand on the boy's shoulder. "Go on. Tell him everything you know."

The words spilled out of Burl, about the other boys asking about the store and about his attempt to break in and that he was now working to pay off the window he broke.

At the officer's raised eyebrows, Ian spoke up. "These boys

are considerably older than Burl and coerced him into doing it. I didn't report it, as Burl was willing to make restitution."

The officer narrowed his eyes at Burl for a moment. "You're a fortunate boy that Mr. MacGregor is so generous."

Burl stood straighter. "Yes, sir."

"Now tell me the full names of these boys."

"Sebastian Phillips and Murphy. . .Murphy? Everyone just calls him Murphy. I don't know his first name, but the school knows."

The officer exchanged a look with Ian. The officer had recognized Phillips as Ian had. Could the boy be the son of the prominent banker? Why would he break into Ian's store? Or anyone else's store? He obviously didn't need money.

The officer's features softened. "Thank you, son. You've been very helpful."

"I never wanted nothin' bad to happen to Mr. Jackson."

The officer nodded. "I'm going to head right over to the school and see if these boys are in class."

Ian heard a commotion on the stairs then saw two men pass by with a stretcher between them. The officer left up the stairs, and Ian followed the men.

Alice moved away from Conner and the doctor to make room.

Ian helped the other three men lift the unconscious Conner onto the stretcher. Then he followed them and the doctor up the stairs and out the front door.

The men slid Conner into the back of the ambulance. One of the men climbed in with him and pulled the doors shut. The horses pulled away and broke into a hurried clip.

The doctor clamped a hand on his shoulder. "You can notify his family?"

"He doesn't have any around here."

"You want a ride to the hospital?"

"I have to get back to my store. I'll come later."

"Have the nurse call for me when you get there, and I'll let you know his full condition."

"Thank you, Doctor."

The doctor climbed into his buggy and took off at a faster clip than the ambulance.

When Ian got back downstairs, he found Alice sweeping broken glass into a pile. "You don't have to do that."

Alice drew in a startled breath. "I thought you'd gone with Mr. Jackson."

"I can't leave the store open like this."

"Burl and I will be here."

"What if those boys come back?" He wouldn't risk anyone else, especially Alice.

"They may be reckless, but I doubt they're stupid enough to come back here so soon. They wouldn't dare show their faces here now that the other stores are open and people are traveling up and down the sidewalk."

"You're right. I'll wait an hour or so, give the doctor a chance to fully examine him."

Burl came up to them. "Fred isn't anywhere in the store. Are you sure they didn't hurt her?"

Fred hadn't seemed hurt, but then Ian's main concern had been Conner. "She probably got out through the open door."

"She could be lost and scared." Burl looked like he was going to start crying again.

"She'll be fine. Remember Mr. Jackson found her on her own before. She'll get along until we can go look for her."

"I'm lookin' outside."

"Don't go far," Alice said.

"If you're fine sweeping, I'm going to see if they took anything in addition to all the damage they did." That included the damage to Conner as well as his store, but he didn't want to distress her any more by reminding her of Conner's injuries. "The officer wants to know if they stole anything."

She nodded. "It's good to keep busy."

He nodded.

Burl came back in with tears on his cheeks again. "She's not anywhere."

"We'll look for her later. Why don't you help your sister by holding the dustpan?" He hoped to distract the boy from the dog's plight for a little while.

He, too, needed a distraction. He hadn't been thrilled at having a dog in his store, but Fred was quiet and didn't bother his customers—most didn't even know she was there. The little mutt had grown on him. He went to the door and peeked out the opening in hopes Fred had returned. No scruffy face looked up at him.

ten

With all the windows open, Alice kept her jacket and shawl on. Mr. MacGregor had said he'd stop by the glazier's on his way to the hospital and arrange for the windows to be replaced. She heard a thump next door and jumped. Every small sound was giving her the jitters.

She wished now she hadn't agreed to let Burl go with Mr. MacGregor, but she knew he needed to know Mr. Jackson would be all right. Burl felt guilty even though it wasn't his fault.

She'd cleaned up all the glass inside and out, even cleaned the glass from the display case counters that had been broken. She wished there was more to keep her busy while Mr. MacGregor and Burl were out. The image of Mr. Jackson unconscious on the floor haunted her.

The break-in had shaken her more than she realized even though she wasn't here, probably because of Mr. Jackson's being injured so badly. She bowed her head for the tenth time that morning to pray for his healing.

A throat clearing startled her, and she squeaked.

"Sorry to scare you, miss." The officer who'd been there earlier walked toward her.

She took a slow breath to calm herself. It did little good. "I'm just a little jumpy."

The officer nodded. "I'd reckon so after the goings-on here this morning."

"May I help you with something?" She put her hands on the edge of the counter, and her fingers curled through where the glass should have been. She removed them.

"I'm looking for Mr. MacGregor."

"He's at the hospital inquiring after Mr. Jackson."

"So you haven't heard anything on his condition?"

"Not yet." She didn't know what to do with her hands so just ended up wringing them together. "But I've been praying all day for him."

"I'm heading over to the hospital later today to see if I can talk to him."

"Do you think he'll be awake?"

"He'd better, or those boys will be in a lot more trouble than they already are." He paused. "Can you tell Mr. MacGregor that we think it might be those two boys? When I went to the school to have a talk with them, they both jumped out the classroom window and ran off. I went to the banks where their fathers work and stationed men at each of their homes."

"You didn't catch them?"

"Not yet, but it's only a matter of time." He headed toward the door. "Tell him I'll stop by at the end of the day to update him and to find out if anything is missing."

"Oh, wait. I almost forgot. There were stolen medicines." She took a slip of paper from beside the cash register. "He asked me to give this to you if you stopped by."

He glanced through the list. "Thank you. If we find them with any of these, it will make it a sure go that they were the ones. Have a good day." He tipped his hat and left.

She went back to the potbelly stove and warmed herself there. A few minutes later, she jumped at the bell over the front door. She took a calming breath and met the glazier measuring the front door window.

"Hello, miss. I'm just going to take a few measurements then board up these drafty air holes." He was a middle-aged man with curly black hair.

"Is there anything I can help you with?"

"Thank you. No. Bobby's right outside."

Another man with curly dark hair poked his head in through one of the window openings and waved at her.

"Oh, good."

She jumped at the voice behind her and spun around, her heart pounding.

"I'm sorry." Mr. MacGregor came over to her. "I didn't mean to scare you. We came through the upstairs and down the back staircase."

"You didn't scare me." He had, but she didn't want him to feel bad. She was really glad they were both back. She wanted to run into his arms but didn't. "I'm just a little jumpy. How's Mr. Jackson?"

Burl stepped forward. "He's real banged up, but he's doing okay. He talked to us then fell asleep."

That was a relief. She turned to Mr. MacGregor for more information.

"He has a broken arm, three broken ribs, and a concussion. With rest, he should recover fine. They're keeping him overnight. I'll take him back to my house tomorrow so he can rest comfortably while he convalesces."

"I'm glad to hear he'll recover. I've been praying for him."

"As have I."

"Did Fred come back while we was gone?" Burl asked.

She shook her head. "I'm sorry. I haven't seen her."

Burl turned to Mr. MacGregor. "We have to go look for her. You promised we would."

"Let me talk to the glazier and see when they'll be finished. We'll go after they have everything boarded up."

"That long? What if she's hurt or scared?"

Alice put a hand on his shoulder. "Burl, it'll have to wait just a little longer."

Mr. MacGregor put a hand on his other shoulder. "If we help them hold the boards, it will go faster."

Burl and Mr. MacGregor went to help, and Alice went back to the potbelly stove. She'd been cold so long that she felt as though she'd never warm up. But at least she didn't feel so jumpy.

A little while later, Burl ran back to where she stood. "We're gonna look for Fred now."

Mr. MacGregor joined them. "They've left. They'll be back tomorrow to put in the windows. The counters will take a little longer to repair."

"Let's go." Burl tugged down his cap.

"I put a CLOSED sign on the outside of the door. Would you like to come with us to search for Fred?"

It would be good to get out and walk about, but the heat promised far more satisfaction. "I'm going to warm up a bit and then walk home if you don't need me here."

"Wait until I return. I don't want you walking alone while those two boys are still out there."

"Why would they come after me?" He was just being ridiculous.

"Why would they go after Conner? They weren't after him, but he got in their way. Promise me you won't go anywhere until I get back, or I won't leave."

"Come on, Alice. Say you'll stay here. Please."

"I do have my knitting bag with me."

Burl beamed at her.

"And don't open the door for *anyone*. I have a key."

"But—" She cut herself off. It was no use arguing with these two. "Hurry back. I hope you find her well." Watching Burl walk away with Mr. MacGregor warmed her heart. He'd been good for her brother. And for her. She prayed that they would find the poor dog in good shape and quickly. And that those boys wouldn't catch up to them.

⛬

Ian rubbed his face, chilly in the brisk afternoon air. He and Burl had been at it for going on an hour and were still no closer to finding Fred. He had no idea where to look. The dog could be anywhere in the city by now. This effort was futile, but how did he tell Burl that? The dog would probably find her own way back.

"I'm gonna check down this alleyway." Burl headed into the shadowy corridor.

"Stay in the middle where I can keep an eye on you." He followed the boy.

"Fred! Here, Fred!"

Did the dog even know her name? She'd probably been kicked around by people who tried to get rid of her and shoo her away all her life, so she wasn't likely to come when called.

But wait a minute. That could be it. Fred had been a stray. She would have had to have found food someplace to stay alive. Maybe someone at one of the restaurants had fed her scraps or at the very least remembered shooing her away. He headed for the nearest one.

"Where are we goin'? Did you find her?" Burl's voice cracked, whether from stress or growing up, Ian couldn't tell.

"I have an idea." He went to the alley first to see if she might be rummaging in the garbage for food scraps. The kitchen door sat slightly ajar. He pulled it halfway open. "Pardon me."

A man with a dirty meat cleaver came over. "I don't give no handout to no bummers. Be gone with you." He waved the cleaver at them.

"We aren't looking for handouts. We are looking for a dog."

"No dogs around here. I'd run 'em off if they chanced to come around. Don't need that kind of trouble around my kitchen."

"Maybe you saw this dog and ran her off. She's a ruddy brown, about this big." He held his hand about eighteen inches apart. "A little mangy looking. Definitely has a streak of terrier in her."

"Haven't seen it."

Someone yelled at the man.

"I'm comin'." Without another word, the man pulled the door closed.

The next two places were much the same. Maybe this

wasn't such a good idea. They would circle this block then start the return trip to his store on different streets than those they'd taken earlier, looking as they went. He wanted to get back before dark and before Alice decided to walk home alone after all.

"There's another one." Burl pointed to the Green Pasture across the street.

It wasn't on their way, but they searched the alley and were greeted by a low growl. A massive dog had something in its mouth, and it was cornered. Ian pushed Burl against the building, and the dog darted away. Fred would be no match for that dog. She'd likely stay away from this place. "Let's go."

"Aren't we gonna knock on the kitchen door and ask about Fred?" Burl sounded hurt.

"It wouldn't hurt." As Ian turned, he noticed an even bigger dog than the other lying down with its head resting on its huge paws in the entrance to the alley. He pressed them both back against the wall. If Ian remembered correctly, that was a Great Dane.

The dog crawled forward a few feet, gave them a furtive glance, then trotted to the kitchen door and scratched.

The door cracked open and a burly voice said, "Tiny, it is so good to see you. Wait here." The man had a German accent.

The dog sat, and its tail brushed the ground as it moved back and forth.

The man returned. "This chicken is too old for me to serve to the customers, but it is still good for you." He held the meat out on his upturned hand, and Tiny gingerly took it from his palm. This dog was clearly not a threat.

Ian stepped forward. "Excuse me, sir."

The man studied him as he and Burl approached. "You are obviously not a beggar." Then he squinted at Burl. "But you could be."

"We're lookin' for a dog," Burl piped up.

The man smiled and pointed to Tiny. "You found one."

"No. Not that big." Burl described Fred.

"That sounds like my Angel."

"She's your dog?" Burl sounded disappointed.

"No more than Tiny is. Most of the strays run in a pack and find food together. A few are stragglers, and I feed them now and then when we have scraps or old food that has not gone bad yet but is not fit to feed people."

Burl shifted his feet. "Have you seen Fred—I mean Angel today, sir?"

"Not today. But then it is not Saturday. She's my usual Saturday customer, but I have not seen her for nearly a month. I hope nothing bad has happened to her."

Ian hoped so, too. "My employee brought her home and has been training her to dispose of the rat problem I have at my store."

The man nodded. "I imagine she would be good at that. A dog likes to feel useful. I am glad she got a good home."

"But she's lost!" Burl squealed.

"There was a bit of trouble at my store this morning. I think she got scared and ran away."

Compassion creased the German man's eyes. "I have not seen her, but if I do, I will hide her in a box in the back until you come for her. I like to see a good dog like Angel get a fine home with a boy to play with."

"Oh, she doesn't live with me. She lives with Mr. Jackson at the store, but I see her every day and play with her. Mr. Jackson was hurt and he's in the hospital."

"I am sorry to hear that. I will keep a watch for Angel."

Ian felt something gently nudging his hand. Looking down, he saw Tiny maneuvering his large head under it. He scratched the dog behind the ear.

"Looks like Tiny favors you." The man laughed then told them about a couple of other restaurants that might have fed Fred.

The problem was that those places took them farther away from his store. "We will ask at these two restaurants then go straight back to your sister."

Burl nodded.

Fred had not been seen at either place.

"Let's ask down there." Burl pointed to the fish market that was all but closed for the day and headed off for it.

After that, he would have to call it a day even if Burl protested. He just hated to disappoint Burl by returning without Fred.

The man at the near booth scrubbed the whiskers on his fleshy chin. "That sounds like the mongrel I run off not more than a half hour ago."

Burl let out a squeak. "You shouldn't have done that. She's a good dog."

"Which way did she go?"

He pointed. "Thataway."

"Thanks." He took off after Burl.

Burl called to Fred over and over. Fred came around a building limping toward them with one front paw raised. Burl ran to her and scooped her up. She whined.

Ian took up the paw she'd been favoring. Blood caked the pad. "Let's get her back to the store and fix this up."

It was dark by the time they reached the store. Mr. Lansky's street-level store was closed, so Ian and Burl, with Fred tucked inside the boy's coat, took the side entrance stairs to the sidewalk below. He unlocked his door. It was dark inside. "Alice?"

No reply.

His stomach clenched. "Wait here. I'll get a light." He headed for the back. *Lord, please let Alice be safe.*

A slight glow emanated from the potbelly stove. He opened the door, lit a slender stick, and held it to a lamp nearby.

eleven

Ian held the lamp high so it shed light about the whole room. A half-knitted scarf lay on the chair near the stove. Where was Alice? He didn't see anything newly broken or disturbed.

Burl came back with Fred still in his coat. "Where should I put her so we can fix her foot?" Burl didn't seem to notice that Alice was missing.

Ian moved the knitting. "Sit here with her. I'll be right back." He didn't want Burl to know he was concerned about Alice. Let the boy just worry over the dog.

Ian went back to the front of the store and looked around all the counters. He was relieved that Alice wasn't lying on the floor somewhere. He stepped into Conner's private room. There lay Alice on top of the bed, sleeping peacefully. Ian's pent-up fear escaped in a breath. *Thank You, Lord.* He knelt beside her, reluctant to wake her.

"Mr. MacGregor," Burl yelled from the other room.

Alice stirred and opened her eyes. "You're back. I must have nodded off. I suddenly got so tired, I decided to lie down for a minute."

He helped her sit up. "We found Fred."

"Good." She rubbed her face.

"She's hurt."

"Mr. MacGregor?" Burl's call was more urgent this time.

"Coming." He helped Alice up.

"What can I do to help?"

He followed her out to the other room where Burl sat with Fred. "Get a bowl of warm water, please, and any clean cloths you can find."

They soaked Fred's foot in warm water to remove the dried

blood and found a piece of glass in her pad. Ian pulled it out with a pair of tweezers. "She must have picked this up when she ran out the door." He wrapped her foot with a strip of clean cloth.

Alice put her knitting into her bag. "We need to be heading home. Grandpa will be wondering what happened to us."

He stood from where he'd laid Fred on a blanket on the floor near the stove. "I'll walk you home."

"That's not necessary." She pulled on her coat.

"Until they catch those boys, I'd feel better if I did." Who knows what they might do next?

"I'm stayin' here with Fred." Burl lay on the floor by the dog, stroking her gently.

"No, Burl. We need to get home." She held out his coat.

Ian gave the boy a hand up. "I'll stay here with Fred over night. She'll be fine."

As they walked up the exterior stairs to ground level, he could immediately feel eyes on him as though someone were watching them. He looked around.

"What's wrong?" Alice asked.

He saw no one. "Nothing." He didn't want to alarm either her or Burl, but he couldn't shake the feeling of being followed. They reached her apartment without incident.

"I was beginning to worry about the two of you." Arthur crossed over to them from the kitchen area.

"Ma." Miles came over with his arms raised, and Alice lifted him.

Ian took Alice's coat and hung it on the back of a chair. "It's been a very long day. I'll let Alice and Burl fill you in on what all happened."

"You're staying for supper. I cooked."

He rubbed the back of his neck. He wanted to. "Thank you for the offer, but I need to get back and make sure Fred isn't trying to pull off her bandage."

He headed back for his store with the same feeling of being watched and followed, but he never saw anyone. Was it his imagination? Or was someone very sneaky?

He locked himself inside his store and went back to check on Fred. The blanket was vacant. He checked in Conner's room. Fred lay curled up in the middle of the bed. "Is that where you usually sleep? Or are you taking advantage of your master being gone?"

Fred looked up at him with sad eyes.

"Very well. You can stay."

Fred laid her head back down.

Tonight he'd sleep here at the store to look after Fred and to make sure no one else tried to get in.

≈

The next morning on the way to work, Burl pulled Alice toward the hospital. "I wanna see Mr. Jackson."

She was anxious to see how he was doing as well; then she could let Mr. MacGregor know when they arrived at the store. They asked for Mr. Jackson at the nurses' desk.

The nurse gave her a gentle smile and said, "He's in the second room on the left. The doctor's with him."

Alice thanked her and went down the hall, trying to keep her shoes from thumping on the polished wood floors. The first room on the right was large and had eight white iron beds down each side, half of which appeared to be empty. Burl veered off to the room on the left. Four beds occupied this smaller room, along with two patients and a doctor. It was nice that Mr. Jackson—or was it Mr. MacGregor—could afford a semiprivate room. The man in the bed by the door lay curled and asleep. Just inside, she stopped and held Burl back as well. She didn't want to interrupt the doctor at Mr. Jackson's bedside by the window.

The doctor turned. "Come in."

She walked to the edge of the white-railed bed with Burl. "How is he?"

"An angel." Mr. Jackson smiled at her then turned to the doctor. "Am I dead?"

"No, you aren't dead." The doctor wrote on the chart he held. "I'm making a note that they not bury you yet."

Mr. Jackson reached out his good arm to her. "Marry me."

The doctor smiled and turned to her. "Between the concussion and the pain medicine, he's a little confused. Keep your visit short. He won't stay awake much longer." The doctor walked out.

Alice was going to ignore his proposal. He probably didn't know what he'd asked anyway. "Mr. Jackson, I'm glad to see that you're all right."

He gave her a lopsided smile, put his arm back down, and closed his eyes.

"Did he die?" Burl whispered.

"No, he's just sleeping. We should go."

The doctor stood at the nurses' desk.

"Doctor, when does Mr. Jackson get to go home?" Mr. MacGregor would want to know.

The doctor handed the chart to the nurse and turned to Alice. "Does he have someone at his home who can watch over him night and day for the next couple of days?"

"Not both night and day. He lives alone."

"Then I'd like to keep him here one more night where the nurses can look after him."

"Thank you, Doctor." Mr. Jackson shouldn't mind staying in the hospital where nurses would care for him. Then he could propose to one of them.

The doctor turned to leave then turned back to her. "Oh, if you need a witness that he proposed marriage, just let me know."

She definitely wouldn't be needing that.

Burl was quiet as they walked then finally he said, "Are you gonna marry Mr. Jackson?"

Of all the questions. "Of course not."

"But you didn't say no."

"Mr. Jackson didn't know what he was saying."

"What if he did? Know what he was sayin'." Burl turned and walked sideways. "Would you marry him?"

She looked directly at him. "No, Burl."

"Why not?"

"Because I don't like him that way. He's a friend."

Burl started walking backward. "But what about Mr. MacGregor?"

"Would you turn around? You'll trip." This was none of Burl's concern.

He turned back around. "Would you? Iffin he asked?"

"No." Her chest tightened. She would not look at him. "He's a friend, too." But those words didn't seem quite right.

"Why not?"

"I'm not marrying anyone." That should close this matter.

"Why not?"

Exasperated, she sighed heavily. "Because I don't want to get married."

"Grace, at school, said that all girls wanna get married."

"I was married once." She just wanted to get off this topic. "Can we talk about something else or nothing at all?"

"I bet Mr. MacGregor would marry you iffin you asked him."

"Burl! Stop it this instant. I'm not—I wouldn't—" She didn't know what to say.

She stopped short at the pharmacy door. Or rather a few feet back from the door. It looked like a small horse was lying in front of the door on his side with his legs stretched out.

"Tiny!" Burl knelt down beside the beast.

"Burl, be careful!"

"Tiny's a nice dog." Burl scratched the dog's chest, and it rolled onto its back.

That was a dog? She'd never seen anything like it. Its legs had to be two and a half feet long. She knocked on one of the boards that served as a window.

Footsteps, then the door opened.

"Hello." Mr. MacGregor smiled at her then looked down. "What's he doing here?"

"He was here when we came," Burl said. "Can we keep him?"

"Burl. We can't have a huge thing like that at our apartment." She'd never be able to feed it. "And I'm sure Mr. MacGregor doesn't want him."

Tiny turned his head and looked up at Mr. MacGregor with big, soulful brown eyes.

Mr. MacGregor knelt down and scratched the dog's chest. "Are you who was following me last night?"

Her stomach clenched at the thought. "You were—we were followed last night? Is that why you kept looking around?"

"I never saw anything. Just sensed it." He stood. "It must have been Tiny."

"What if it wasn't?"

He gave her a direct look. "It was." Then he looked down at Burl. "Bring him in for now. He doesn't make a very useful doormat. No one can get inside."

"Come on, boy." Burl patted his legs, and Tiny flipped over and onto his feet. "How's Fred? Did she leave her bandage alone? Did she eat? Did she drink? Can she walk okay?"

"Burl, take a breath." She took a breath for him. Would he never stop this morning?

Mr. MacGregor smiled at her. "Fred's fine. She's on the blanket by the stove. Why don't you take Tiny back there?" In a softer voice only for her he said, "That will get that horse out of the front and keep it from scaring any customers."

"You aren't going to keep it, are you?"

He shrugged. "It can't hurt to have him in the back just for today."

"He'll think he's come home and never leave." Mr. MacGregor had that comforting effect on people.

He looked at her sideways. "I thought you liked dogs. You never said anything against Fred."

"I love dogs, but Fred's not going to eat Mr. Jackson out of house and home. I can only imagine how much a huge dog like that would eat." Likely more than her whole family. But Mr. MacGregor was free to do as he wished.

Burl came back out. "Tiny licked Fred's head and lay down by her. They're friends. Fred's gonna like havin' Tiny here."

"I think it's you who are going to like having Tiny here. And I doubt Mr. MacGregor is going to keep him."

"Then Mr. Jackson will." Burl said it as if it were all settled.

She just shook her head. As long as she didn't get talked into taking the beast home. She had no room. "We went to the hospital on our way over."

"How was Conner?"

"Fine. The doctor wants to keep him another night if there's no one to look after him both day and night."

"I'll see to him. It's the least I can do. Was he awake or talking or anything?"

Burl stepped between them. "Mr. Jackson asked Alice to marry him."

Mr. MacGregor's eyes widened.

Not this again, and not in front of Mr. MacGregor, of all people. "He wasn't lucid. He also thought I was an angel."

"You do look like an angel."

She sighed. "I do not."

"So what was your answer?"

She knit her eyebrows together. "To what?"

"If you would marry Conner?" He gazed at her intently.

She huffed. "It wasn't a real question, and he likely won't even remember he asked it."

"He's a handsome man. You could do worse."

"I'm not interested in marrying Mr. Jackson."

Something in the twitch of his mouth told her that pleased him.

"She won't even marry you," Burl piped up.

"Burl!"

"Well, that's what you said."

The pleasure on Mr. MacGregor's face washed away. "It's not personal. I don't plan to marry anyone. I. . .I'm going to see how Fred's doing." Flustered, she walked to the back. Tears burned the back of her eyes. Fred limped over to her and whined. Alice scratched Fred's head. Tiny came over and sat in front of her. She gave him a scratch behind the ear, as well.

It was silly to feel like crying. She willed the tears away. She had no reason to cry. No reason at all.

twelve

Late in the afternoon, Ian used his telephone for the second time in two days and called for a taxi. He would see Alice and Burl safely home then retrieve Conner from the hospital unless he preferred to stay an extra night. "The taxi should be here momentarily."

Alice came from the back, buttoning up her coat. "Burl and I can make it home on our own. You go straight to the hospital."

How many times did he have to tell her? "Until those boys are caught, I'm not taking any chances. Burl, will you get Fred? She can't stay here alone tonight." He wondered if that had been Arthur's coat. He doubted it was her late husband's.

He locked the front door with its fresh new window and guided Alice and Burl around the corner and up the stairs. Tiny lumbered along behind him.

"What about Tiny?" Burl knelt beside the huge dog with his arms wrapped around his neck.

"It's time for Tiny to head back to wherever he came from." He turned Tiny loose and helped Alice into the black, hardtopped taxi. One of the horses nickered and pawed the ground. Ian waited for Burl to scramble in before climbing aboard himself and closing the door.

Burl craned his neck to look out the rear window. "Will Tiny be all right? He looks sad."

"Tiny will be fine."

Alice patted Burl's knee. "Turn around."

Burl did and looked about the interior. "I never rode in no carriage before. You must be rich."

He wouldn't call himself rich, but neither was he a pauper,

113

and he wasn't prepared to comment on it. He would let the boy and Alice draw their own conclusions about his bank account.

Alice jerked her head toward Burl. "That is enough. You will not talk about such things. It's rude."

She turned to him. "I'm very sorry."

When the taxi stopped at Alice's apartment building and Ian got out to help her down, Tiny came up and sat beside him.

"Look! Tiny followed us." Burl jumped down and hugged the dog. "Can we keep him, Alice? Please?"

Ian saw her grit her teeth. "Absolutely not. We don't have room for him, and what would we feed him?"

"He can have half of my food. I don't need so much."

"No."

"I almost have the window paid for. I can buy food for him." Burl turned eyes almost as sad as Tiny's on her.

Ian put a hand on the boy's shoulder. "Sorry, pal. I think I've decided to keep him after all. I'll bring him to the store, and you can see him there."

Alice seemed grateful at not having to argue with Burl further over Tiny's welfare and gifted Ian with a smile. That made it all worthwhile. But what on earth was he going to do with a mammoth-sized dog?

He asked the driver to wait for him and walked Alice and Burl upstairs. He then went to the hospital. When he strode up to Conner's white iron bed, the police officer standing by the bed looked up.

"I'm glad you're here. Mr. Jackson was just about to convey what transpired yesterday morning."

Conner sat on the edge of the bed dressed, waiting to be taken home. "Like I started to say, I'd just finished shaving when I heard the crash. Glass breaking. It hadn't been that long since I'd heard that sound. I thought it couldn't be Burl. He'd have no reason. Fred ran out to the front, barking like mad." Conner stopped and put his hand to his bandaged head.

Ian went to Conner's side and helped him lie back down. "Do you want us to get the doctor?"

Conner shook his head. "I'll be fine. I don't want to give them any reason to keep me here." He took several slow, deep breaths. "More glass broke. They threw something toward Fred—a bone, I think. I told Fred no and called her to me. There were two of them. Boys. With baseball bats."

"Could you identify them?" The officer eyed Conner cautiously.

"Sure." Conner gave a quick description of the boys.

"Then what happened?"

"They'd smashed all the front windows. I hollered at them. One of them smashed a display counter and said, 'Let's get him.' They came at me together. I remember raising my arm." He started to lift his casted arm, but the effort seemed too much. "I reached for the one boy's bat and got ahold of the end of it. I remember hearing a *crack* as the other boy's bat connected with my arm. I figured if I could get one of their bats, I could take them. There was searing pain in my left arm. I felt a jerk; then the wind was knocked out of me. I don't remember anything after that. Not even hitting the floor." He closed his eyes and took several labored breaths.

Was he all right? Maybe he shouldn't leave today. "I'm calling for the doctor."

Conner latched on to his arm lightning fast. "Don't. I'll be fine. Just take me home."

The officer's face held concern. "That's all for now. If you think of anything else, let me know. We think we know who these boys are. I'll have you identify them when we catch them."

The officer turned from Conner to him. "Make sure he rests."

He nodded, and the officer left as a nurse came in.

The pretty young nurse smiled brightly at Conner. "You all ready to leave us?"

Conner mustered a halfhearted smile. "Sure am."

"I agree with the doctor. I think you should stay one more day. I'll take good care of you."

The muscle in Conner's jaw worked back and forth. "I'm sure you would, but I'll rest better in my own bed. Besides, you have patients much worse off then me that need your attention."

The doctor came in then. "Did Nurse Sybil tell you I'd feel better if you stayed one more day?"

Conner sat up in the bed holding his ribs. "I just want to get home to my own bed."

"Do you have someone there who can look after you for the next couple of days in case there are any complications?"

Conner nodded. "My good friend Fred will be with me at all times."

Ian squelched the sudden desire to laugh. The dog wasn't going to be much help if something happened, but Conner desperately wanted out of the hospital for some reason, so he wouldn't spoil it.

The doctor released Conner, and Ian took him out to the waiting taxi.

Conner climbed in and sat on the seat next to Fred. Fred sidled up to him. Conner lifted Fred's wrapped paw. "Looks like we're a matched pair."

Ian told the driver where to go, and the taxi lurched into motion. "I'm taking you to my house, where I can keep an eye on you."

"That's not necessary. I'll be fine at the store."

"Fred won't be much help. It'll only be for a couple of days."

Conner nodded. Then glancing next to Ian, he frowned. "Am I seeing things, or is there a moose sitting next to you?"

Ian petted Tiny's head as the dog sat on the seat next to him with his front paws on the floor of the carriage. "This is Tiny. Burl and I went out looking for Fred yesterday, and he followed me home."

Conner nodded again then rested his head against the back of the carriage, looking more relaxed than he had at the hospital.

&

"Mr. Jackson, let me help you with that. You're having another one of those headaches, aren't you?"

Ian watched from across the store as Alice tried to take the ledger book from Conner.

Conner frowned. "I'm not an invalid." He had convalesced at Ian's house over the weekend and was itching to get back to work. He hated being idle.

"You have a broken arm and broken ribs."

"Mrs. Dempsey, I am painfully aware of my shortcomings. But I'd rather get along on my own." Conner gave her the ledger and walked to the back room.

Alice stared over at Ian. "I was only trying to help."

Ian left Burl with his arithmetic problems and came over to her. "I know. It hurts a man's pride to be incapacitated, even just a little. If he needs help, I'll see that he gets it. I won't let him overexert himself." He headed to the back and found Conner. "Are you all right?"

Conner turned on him but spoke softly. "I'll not have her fussing over me." He looked as much in pain as angry.

"She's only trying to help. I'd think you'd be grateful."

"She's your woman, Ian," Conner said a bit louder than he'd intended then lowered his voice again. "I'll not be getting between the two of you."

"She's not exactly my woman, though I wish it were otherwise." It was good to know that his friend held these strong convictions.

"Close enough. I'll not have her start developing feelings for me—not that I think she would—but if I have to be rude to keep her away from me, I will."

He didn't think it would come to that. "Is that why you were in a hurry to get out of the hospital? Were the nurses *fussing* over you?"

"I just wanted to rest." Conner raked a hand through his hair. "I'd wake up, and one of them would be standing next to my bed. Just staring. Got to where I was afraid to close my eyes at all. That was when the officer and you showed up. I never did one thing to make those nurses think I was interested in a one of them."

"I don't know about the nurses, but you may have given Alice cause to think you were interested." He had to smile.

Conner looked him directly in the eyes, unblinking. "I have only ever been cordial and polite. I have never led her to think I was interested in her. Romantically that is."

Under normal circumstance that was true. "You weren't quite yourself with the pain and the medication you were on when you were at the hospital. Alice and Burl stopped by to visit you the morning after you were injured."

Conner squinted his eyes in concentration. "I think I vaguely remember seeing someone that could have been Mrs. Dempsey. I thought I was seeing an angel."

"You proposed marriage to that angel."

Conner's eyes widened. "I did no such thing. I—I couldn't have."

"You did. The doctor and Burl are witnesses."

Conner rubbed his hand on the back of his neck. "I don't remember doing that."

"She said you wouldn't."

"You have to believe me when I say that I have no interest in her." Conner looked near panic. "She's a lovely woman—for you, but I have no interest in her aside from my friendship with you."

"I know, and I appreciate that. I think she'll leave you be. I told her your pride was hurt."

"But what about the proposal? Should I talk to her?"

"She didn't believe it was an authentic proposal. She told Burl that she wouldn't marry you."

Conner let out a huge sigh.

"She also said she wouldn't marry me or anyone else. It seems she plans to stay single the rest of her life." Ian sighed.

"She could change her mind. You could change her mind."

He wasn't so sure about that.

Burl ran back to them. "Mr. MacGregor, the policeman's here. Alice says to come."

Both he and Conner headed to the front.

The officer shook hands with each of them. "It's good to see you're doing well."

"Thank you."

"We found the two boys down by the docks. They were trying to sell the medicines they stole. They claim to have found them and don't know where they came from. If you're feeling up to it, I'd like to take you down to the jail and see if you recognize them as the two who attacked you."

"Gladly. Let me get my coat."

It appeared that Conner wanted out of the store right then as badly as he'd wanted out of the hospital.

❧

The next day, Alice noticed that Mr. Jackson was ignoring her, even avoiding her. That wasn't like him. He was usually polite and friendly. As Mr. MacGregor said, his body wasn't the only thing injured by those boys. She went back to doing. . .nothing. Once she'd scrubbed all the shelves and given the whole store a good cleaning, there wasn't much for her to do. She didn't know the medicines, so Mr. MacGregor and Mr. Jackson helped all the customers that came. And when Mr. MacGregor wasn't helping a customer, he was teaching Burl. She would gladly learn about the medicines, but how with everyone so busy? Everyone but her. She pushed the broom around to occupy herself.

Mr. MacGregor was going to realize soon that her work here was completed and that he and Mr. Jackson could easily keep up. He would see that he didn't need her anymore. She loathed the thought of searching for another job. But maybe she wouldn't have to.

She stood the broom in the corner and crossed the store. "Mr. Jackson?"

He jumped and spun around.

"I'm sorry. I didn't mean to startle you."

"You didn't. I wasn't expecting you to be right behind me."

"I've been wanting to speak to you since you got out of the hospital."

He glanced down toward Mr. MacGregor and Burl. "Mrs. Dempsey, I understand that I might have said things to you when you brought Burl to the hospital."

"Mr. Jackson, please don't worry about any of that."

"I can't help it. I didn't mean to"—he lowered his voice— "propose to you."

She whispered back, "I know."

"Well the thing is, if you're thinking that there's something between the two of us, um. . ."

"I'm not. You were barely awake and in a lot of pain. I'm surprised you even knew anyone was standing there."

He seemed only mildly comforted by her words. He rubbed the back of his neck with his good hand. "If you're hoping I'll propose again. . ."

"I'm not. I have no interest in marrying again. To you or anyone else."

The concern over the proposal slipped away, and Mr. Jackson raised his eyebrows in interest. "No one? Why not? I'm sorry, that was too personal a question."

It was a personal question and bold of him to ask, but she didn't mind answering. "Marriage didn't agree with me."

"Maybe it was your first husband that was disagreeable." He glanced down the counter toward Mr. MacGregor.

Was he suggesting something? So he'd taken her answering his other question as free rein for him to continue to be bold. She did not want to discuss Mr. MacGregor with him. She would put an end to this. "*Mr. Jackson*, I came over here to ask you if you would teach me about the medicines. I want to be useful now that the store is in good order."

"Ian would be the one to teach you about those."

"As you can see, Mr. MacGregor already has a pupil."

"He would gladly make time for you."

It was best if she didn't spend too much time alone with him.

Mr. Jackson gave her a little bow. "It's time for the dogs to go out."

"It's time for you to rest. I'll take the dogs." Fresh air would be good.

When she returned with the dogs and was hanging up her coat, Mr. MacGregor met her in the back room. "Conner said you are interested in learning about the medicines."

She didn't want to bring to his attention the fact that she was becoming useless. She didn't worry about Burl here. "I thought I could be more useful if I could help customers, as well."

"That's an excellent idea. We'll start tomorrow with your lessons."

Her heart leapt for joy at being able to remain employed at Mr. MacGregor's store, but at the same time, it sank into the pit of her stomach. She would be working closely with Mr. MacGregor. She would have to make sure the relationship remained professional. . .for both of them.

❧

After a month of working for Mr. MacGregor, Alice was starting to feel secure in her job and in the arrangements and beginning to believe that all Mr. MacGregor had said about her being only an employee and wanting to help was true.

Burl was flourishing under his guidance and excelling in his studies. Mr. MacGregor looked up from where he sat at the far end of the long counter instructing Burl and smiled at her. Her stomach did a little flip, and she smiled back.

He excused himself from Burl's side and came over. "I've been meaning to ask you something."

Her stomach sank as if a rock had just been thrown into it.

"I respectfully would like to request that you call me Ian. If that suits you."

Surprisingly it did. She knew she shouldn't accept this advancement in their relationship, but. . . "I can accommodate that request. You may call me Alice if you like. . .Ian."

His smile stretched. "Alice."

He made it sound like a delicacy, and goose bumps rose on her arms.

The bell over the door stole his attention.

The officer strode through the doorway. "I'm so mad I can spit."

What was it now? She followed Mr. Mac—Ian around the counter to where the officer stood.

Mr. Jackson joined them. "What's the problem?"

"The fathers of the boys who broke in here have agreed to pay for all damages if the boys won't go to jail. Both boys are being sent to a military boarding school. Their fathers are friends with the judge."

"So they won't go to jail?" She couldn't believe that. It wasn't just.

The officer shook his head in disgust. "Though if they so much as breathe wrong at the boarding school, they go straight to jail."

Ian frowned. "Where is this school? Far from here I hope."

"Not far enough in my opinion. It's back East."

That was far enough for her.

thirteen

Ian locked the door after Alice and Burl and pulled the shade down.

Conner came up beside him. "You're making progress. I heard her call you Ian, and you're now to call her by her given name."

Ian was grateful for the small step. "But it's a long way from her accepting a marriage proposal."

"So you're sure you want to make her Mrs. Ian MacGregor?"

He liked the sound of that and smiled. "Every day. I'd marry her tomorrow if she were agreeable. I want to get her and her family out of that tenement they're living in."

"Yet you don't want to pressure her and scare her away. How long are you willing to wait?"

"A lifetime. There is no other woman who can fill this need inside my heart." Ian stopped at the knock on the door. He wanted to ignore it, but if someone was in need, he didn't want to turn him away. He rolled up the shade and looked out, then immediately opened the door. "Arthur. Finn. Come in." He looked down the sidewalk for Alice, but she wasn't there. Miles, holding tightly to his grandpa's hand, came in with them.

Conner appeared with two chairs.

He motioned for Arthur to take a seat. "Alice just left."

"I know." Arthur sat.

Finn looked at Conner. "These two need a little privacy."

Conner nodded and took Miles's hand. "You want to see the dogs?"

Miles grinned. "Doggy." The three left for the back.

Arthur motioned to the other chair.

Ian joined him. "What can I do for you?"

"I haven't much time, so I'll get to the point. Marry my granddaughter."

Ian sputtered. He would like nothing better, but even he could tell he had a long way to go to gain her confidence enough to suggest he might propose. "I don't think Alice has known me long enough or likes me well enough for such a proposition."

Arthur drilled his gray gaze into him. "Do you love her?"

He wasn't going to answer that. "Did you talk to her about this?"

Arthur raised his stump arm. "I may not be the man I once was, but I am still patriarch of this family."

"You would force her to marry?"

"Arranged marriages are not completely a thing of the past."

But they weren't as popular as they once were. They certainly were never widely popular with young ladies forced into a loveless marriage. "I have learned that Alice is a self-sufficient woman. She may not take kindly to the issues being forced upon her."

Arthur drew in a deep breath. "You let me worry about that. She'll do as I tell her. I'm an old man. I won't always be around for her. I need to know she'll be looked after when I'm gone."

Ian was sure, given the right circumstances, Alice could do well providing for herself and anyone else in her care. "You'd better ask her first."

Arthur waggled his head back and forth. "Back to my earlier question. Do you love her?"

He stared at the old man, unsure if he should answer. He wished Conner would come in and interrupt, but he knew he wouldn't. "I do." The confession exploded joy in his heart.

"If she agrees, will you marry her?"

He really wanted Conner to return now. He wanted to say

yes but was reluctant to say so for some reason. He felt backed into a corner. Somehow either answer would be wrong.

❧

Alice fetched the remaining dirty dishes off the table. It had been a good day at the store with Ian. She was glad he'd asked her to call him by his given name.

"Alice, sit down." Grandpa patted the table.

"I need to finish cleaning up." She tested the water in the pan to see if it was hot enough to wash the dishes in. Still a bit cool. She wanted to get her chores done so she could finish the scarf she'd started. They sold well at the pharmacy; that was mainly Ian's doing. He pointed out their benefit to nearly every customer.

"Come. Sit. I need to talk to you." Grandpa moved her chair with his foot.

She grabbed her knitting and sat. "What is it?" The needles clicked as she worked.

"I'm not getting any younger."

"Don't talk like that. You aren't that old." Why did he always have to remind her of his age?

"What man lives long enough to meet his great-grandchild?"

She gathered both needles together and covered his hand with one of her own. "A man who has been blessed by the Lord."

Grandpa turned his hand over and squeezed hers. "Alice, look at me. Really look at me. I'm an old man. I'm tired and weary. This old body is barely hanging on. I'm ready to go home to Jesus and see my bonny Erin."

"Grandpa, please don't." She was painfully aware how tired and weary he was. That was why she worked so hard.

He brought her hand to his lips and kissed it. "You live in a dream world, lass. One where I will live forever."

Tears rimmed her eyes. Truth hurt. She didn't want to think about Grandpa dying. "If I think about life without you, it'll be too much. I'll break."

"I know. You take the weight of all of us upon yourself." He released her hand and sat straighter. "That is why I have made a decision. You need someone to help you."

Her tears ebbed. She didn't like the turn his voice had taken. He knew she was not going to like what he was about to tell her. "We're doing just fine."

"Not so well as you like to think. I have decided that you will marry again."

"What? I don't think marriage is a good idea. I didn't do so well picking a husband the first time."

"That's why I'm going to choose for you. Mr. MacGregor will be your husband."

Mr. MacGregor! Somehow this was his doing. Had he been planning this all along? "Shouldn't Mr. MacGregor have a say in this matter?" She would talk to him first and tell him to turn down Grandpa's offer.

"He said yes."

❧

The bell over the door jingled; then the door slammed. Ian looked up from the book he was showing Burl. An icy glare from Alice met him. He was glad that no customers were in the store yet.

She came over. "Burl, change into your old clothes."

"But these are my work clothes."

"You're not staying."

"But I just got here."

"Go."

Burl folded his arms. "I'm learnin'."

Something had upset Alice, and Ian might have a guess at what. It would be best if he didn't aggravate her further. "Burl, do as your sister says." Arthur should have waited.

Burl turned to him. "But—"

"Now."

Burl jumped off the stool and shuffled to the back. "Alice—"

"It's *Mrs.* Dempsey."

So they were back to that. "I can see you're upset." He spoke calmly to help defuse her anger.

"Have you been planning this from the beginning?"

"Planning what?" He knew what but wanted to stall for time to think.

Her face turned red. "Forcing me to marry you?"

"That wasn't my idea. I would never make you do anything you didn't want to do."

"No, you just carefully put all the pieces into place so I'd have no other recourse. You made it so I and my whole family would be completely dependent on you so when marriage came up, I'd fall into your arms with gratitude."

"It's not like that, Alice."

She glowered at his using her first name. He didn't care. She'd offered him the use of it, so he would.

"You gave me a job when you probably didn't need more help here, and you're teaching Burl."

Neither one of those was cause for her anger. "I only wanted to help."

"Did Burl even break into your store, or did the two of you cook that up?"

He could fix this if she would only listen. "Would you just calm down?"

"Now I'm a hysterical woman?"

Just a bit, but he didn't think it would help the situation to say so.

"Maybe you plotted with Miss Morgan to fire me so you could save me by giving me a job and I'd be so grateful. . .I'd. . . oooh." She turned toward the back. "Burl, hurry up!"

"Alice, would you listen to yourself? All this plotting and scheming. I did none of those things you are accusing me of."

She pinned him with a cold blue glare. "You didn't talk to my grandfather about marrying me behind my back?"

"Well, yes I did, but—"

"But nothing."

This wasn't going so well. "You have made me out to be some sort of monster."

"You are no monster; you're worse. You can tell a monster on sight; he looks evil. You came as a friend then betrayed me and stabbed me in the back. I thought you were a nice man. I guess I was wrong."

"Alice, why are you so mad?" Burl had tears in his eyes. "Why are you yellin' at Mr. MacGregor?"

"Come on, Burl. We're leaving."

"I wanna stay." Burl folded his arms.

"You are never to step foot in this store again. Do you understand me?"

Burl's bottom lip quivered, and he nodded.

She pointed a finger at Ian. "Is that understood?"

He just needed a minute to explain how it all had happened and held his hands out from his sides. "Can we sit down and talk about this?"

"Burl is not to be in here again."

She was being unreasonable, but he nodded anyway. Maybe if he agreed with her, she would be amenable to talking this over when she wasn't so upset.

She pointed her finger at Conner who stood behind the far end of the counter, looking as though he were trying to be invisible.

He nodded before she could make her demand.

She put her hand on Burl's shoulder and turned to leave.

He couldn't let her leave like this and grabbed her arm, turning her back around. "I am a nice man. Marriage was your grandfather's idea."

"But you agreed to it."

"Only if you were agreeable."

"Well, I'm not. So you'd better tell my grandfather that the deal is off." She shook loose from his grip and walked out. Burl gave a sorrowful look back with tears on his cheeks. He wiped them away with his shirtsleeve.

The poor boy. She was mad at him, so why couldn't Burl stay? Ian had enjoyed teaching such an eager young mind. He sent up a quick prayer asking what he was to do now and how he could continue to help Alice and her family.

Conner let out a long whistle.

He turned to Conner. "I had a feeling Arthur's proposal was too good to be true."

"Are you going to go after her?"

"I don't think that would be wise in her present state, but I do think I'll go talk to Arthur. Let him know the outcome of his little plan." He'd been making progress with Alice, but thanks to Arthur's little scheme, it was all ruined.

"Won't she be there and be mad at you for being there?"

"I don't think she'll go straight home. She won't want to be this upset when she faces her grandfather. She'll make an effort to look for a new job or go clear her head. Don't you think?"

"The secrets of the feminine mind, what man can fathom? What are you going to tell him?"

"That the wedding is off. Without Alice's consent, I won't force matrimony."

"But you want to marry her, right?"

"Not like this." He headed out the door and found himself quickly at Alice's apartment. He hesitated for a moment before knocking.

After hearing a scuffle of shoe soles on the floor, Miles opened the door with Arthur hobbling close behind.

"Hello, little man." He looked up. "Hello, Arthur."

"Come in." Arthur closed the door behind him and maneuvered himself over to the table and sat. "Please sit."

He took the chair adjacent to the old man. "When Alice arrived at the store this morning, she was in quite a state."

"She told you then."

He leaned on the table. "Arthur, she's not happy with me at

all. She'll never marry me this way."

"She'll simmer down."

"Not on this." He leaned forward on the table. "She ordered Burl never to set foot in my store, and I seriously doubt she will ever come in there again. She does not want to marry me under any circumstances."

"She'll simmer down."

"I don't think so. She thinks I've been planning this from the start." He rubbed the back of his neck. "She thinks I was somehow responsible for her getting fired so she would have to work for me."

"She'll simmer down."

"You didn't see how upset she was."

"She'll simmer down."

He shook his head. "You keep saying that. How can you be so sure?"

"She's just like my Erin, all hot and bothered, but Erin always simmered down and came to her senses." Arthur patted his hand. "You'll see. She'll marry you."

"No, Arthur. I don't want any part of your plan."

"Would you rather see her become another man's wife?"

His eyes widened. "What?"

Arthur smiled. "That's what I thought. You love her."

"But I would never force her to marry me."

"But I would."

The old man must be losing his mind. "Why?"

"I'm old. She needs someone to take care of her."

He made it all sound so easy. "I don't think she sees it that way."

"I need to know that she has a good man to take care of her before I die. It's the least I can do for her if not the only thing." Arthur raised his stump.

"Arthur, I'm sure you have many good years left."

"Only the good Lord knows that for sure."

Ian rubbed a hand over his face. Arthur was exasperating.

He wouldn't listen any more than Alice would. "If something should happen to you, I promise to look after Alice, Burl, and Miles."

"Her husband will do that. Will that be you?"

"You are a stubborn old man."

Arthur smiled. "When I know what's right, I don't back down. Alice takes too much on her slim shoulders. I'll see her married before I die."

No wonder Alice had come to Ian. She knew she couldn't reason with her grandfather.

Arthur looked at him. "Do you agree with me that she would be better off if she were married and had someone to share the burdens with?"

Ian reluctantly nodded.

"Are you going to be the one?"

He didn't want to agree to anything. He was already in enough trouble. "Let's give her some time to cool off and get used to the idea."

"Don't take too much time. I'm not going to live forever."

If a person could postpone dying by a simple act of the will, Arthur would live another eighty or more years.

❧

Alice stopped outside her apartment door and took a deep breath. She'd calmed down considerably since seeing Ian— Mr. MacGregor. She'd put Burl back into school. . .against his will. She was ready to face Grandpa. When he asked why she wasn't at work, she'd tell him that she'd been given the day off. That would give Mr. MacGregor some time to tell him that the wedding was off. She opened the door and was surprised to see Ian sitting at her table.

He stood and dipped his head to her. "Mrs. Dempsey. I was just leaving." He put on his bowler hat, and as he passed her, he said, "It's all taken care of. It is as you wished it. Your final pay and the money for the scarves still at the store are on the table."

An ache ripped open inside her as she watch him walk out the door and out of her life. A part of her wanted to call him back.

"You've made a fine mess. I'll talk to him in a few days and put this all right." Grandpa looked so sad and disappointed in her.

She didn't know what to say. Did she not want Grandpa to bother at all? Or did she want him to make it "all right" in his eyes? She missed Ian already.

She looked at the money on the table. She didn't even want it. She went to her room and closed the door; then she lay across the bed and cried but had no idea why. Was it because of the disappointment on Grandpa's face? Was it because she'd made a fool of herself in front of Ian and yelled at him? Was it because her emotions were just a huge jumble and crying was her only release? Was it because she had to face going back out and searching for a job that wouldn't be there? Or was it because she knew she would eventually have to go crawling back to Ian?

If only everything could go back to the way it was before, when Ian looked at her in that way he did. She'd disappointed Grandpa and hurt Ian. Why did they have to insist she marry Ian?

fourteen

Ian sat at the counter with his ledger book open before him, unable to concentrate. He wasn't even sure if he needed to do anything in the ledger. It had been only a few hours, but he missed her. Nothing else seemed to matter but Alice. He'd do anything to change the events of the past twenty-four hours. *Lord, show me how to fix this and how to help her.*

"I think you have a visitor," Conner said.

He hadn't heard the bell but glanced up anyway. No one. He furrowed his brow at Conner.

Conner pointed toward the door. "Outside."

He looked through door glass and saw Burl. "He's not supposed to be here."

"I think that's why he's standing outside. He knows he's not supposed to come inside."

Smart boy. He went to the door and stepped outside. "Where are you supposed to be?"

Burl shrugged.

If he knew Alice, she'd put him back into school, and he'd say it was about time for lunch. "Shouldn't you be in school?"

"I don't learn nothin' there. I want you to teach me. Alice doesn't have to know that I'm here, not iffin you say it's all right."

He wanted to keep Burl there with him but knew he couldn't—or rather, shouldn't. If he wanted to win her back, he had to abide by her wishes. . .for the time being. "Your sister made it quite clear that she does not want you in my store. You'd best go back to school before you get in trouble."

"Iffin we were to meet on the street or something, we could talk, right? Alice never said nothin' about that."

He had to smile. This boy was going to figure out a way to get what he wanted.

Burl's face brightened. "Like, let's say just after school, iffin I was at the vacant lot up on Fifth Street and you happened to show up, that would be okay because I'm not in your store. I promise not to get into any trouble and go to school iffin you came and brought your books."

No wonder Alice thought he was plotting against her. She had a family of schemers. First Grandpa, now Burl. If she wasn't so stubborn and unyielding, maybe they all wouldn't have to. "I could do for an afternoon walk each day around three." And maybe he could finally train Burl out of using *iffin*.

Burl smiled then started to run off but stopped and turned. "Thanks."

What could it hurt? If it kept Burl out of trouble, that would still be helpful to Alice. He had prayed for a way to help her. He felt lighter somehow just knowing he would be seeing Burl regularly, a small connection to her.

❧

Alice set down her knitting for the sixth time and went to the window. The sun through the glass warmed her face. She could picture Ian at his store trying to convince Mr. Jenkins Sr. to brew the leaves of the cottonwood tree into a tea and put it on a cloth on his hands for his arthritis and to take a syrup for his cough. Mr. Jenkins would buy the syrup for his cough but not the arthritis treatment. Ian would slip the leaves into the old man's pocket when he walked him to the door. Mr. Jenkins wasn't the only customer Ian gave free medicine to or cut the price for. He was a generous man.

"Oh why don't you just go talk to him?" Grandpa growled.

She turned. "Talk to whom?"

"You know good and well. You've been skittering around this apartment for two days. You're worse than a long-tailed cat in a room full of rockers. Git." He waved her away.

She did at least owe Ian an apology for yelling at him the

way she had. She swung on her shawl. "I'll be back in time to make supper."

Grandpa smiled. "Bring company for supper."

"No, Grandpa." She shook her head as she slipped out the door.

Another beautiful day. It seemed Old Man Winter had decided to let Seattle dry out for the past month. The puddles were gone, and the streets were dry. But dark clouds were billowing in from the west, and there was a bite in the air. She pulled her shawl closer. She should have worn her coat. Yes, their streak of fair weather had come to an end. Just when she was beginning to think that spring would come early this year.

She stopped just short of Ian's store. *Lord, give me the strength to face this battle. Help me to hold my tongue. Guard my speech.* She wouldn't even entertain the idea that Ian would give her the job back. Bracing herself for his inevitable disapproval, she opened the door.

Mr. Jackson was helping a customer, but Ian was nowhere in sight. Mr. Jackson raised his eyebrows then finished up the sale. "Mrs. Dempsey, what a pleasant surprise."

Mr. Jackson didn't turn her out immediately. That had to be good. "I'm looking for Mr. MacGregor."

"You are?"

Mr. Jackson looked troubled, and she couldn't figure out why. "Is he here?"

"Ian? No. He stepped out. He might be back soon. Would you like to wait?"

She felt like an unwelcome guest at a fancy birthday party. "I'll try again tomorrow."

"Are you sure? He could be back any minute."

"I'll return another time."

"He'll be sorry he missed you."

She wasn't so sure of that as she left. He'd probably be glad he missed another potential tirade from her. She could use this time to figure out just what to say to him. She walked over a block and headed up the hill but stopped short when she saw Burl walking on the other side of the street.

With Mr. MacGregor!

How dare he go behind her back? Flashes of Oscar deceiving her and gambling away their farm cluttered her head. From the beginning, he'd set out to dupe her. She'd promised herself she would never be that gullible again. Just when she would think she could trust Ian, he'd go behind her back.

"Burl!"

Her brother jerked his head up, and his eyes grew large. "Uh-oh."

Ian looked up at her with wide eyes, then closed them and ducked his head in defeat. The two of them crossed the street. "Go to your sister."

"I don't wanna."

Ian gave him a stern look. "Go."

Burl came to her with a book in his hand. "We wasn't doing nothin' wrong. After school I was just walkin' down the street and I seen Mr. MacGregor. So I stopped to talk. I was only being polite."

"A chance meeting? Is that what you expect me to believe?" She grabbed the corner of the book he held tightly and shook her head. "You expect me to believe you took this route home from school?"

Burl nodded.

"School is twelve blocks in the other direction!"

Burl twisted the toe of his shoe on the sidewalk. "I wanted to get some exercise." He was hopeless.

She expected better out of Ian. "Mr. MacGregor, do you always walk around town with an armload of books?"

He shook his head.

She held out her hand to Burl. "Give me the book."

"Mr. MacGregor gave it to me."

"He can keep it. I want him to have it."

It would be too much of a battle to try to wrestle the book

from Burl. He was getting too big for that. She glared at Ian. "Stay away from my brother. Don't ever see him again." If she couldn't trust him with this small request, how could she trust him with something bigger?

"No, Alice, no!" Burl pulled on her arm.

"Come on. We're going home."

"I want Mr. MacGregor to teach me."

"We'll talk about this at home."

"I hate you." Burl stormed off down the street.

"I really meant no harm." Ian held out his free arm. "I only wanted to help. He said he would stay out of trouble and stay in school like you wanted."

"You went behind my back." Tears threatened her eyes.

"I never meant to."

"But you did. You deceived me. That's what hurts most." She turned and walked away, the ache inside her chest ripping wide open.

&

Ian was glad that there were no customers in his store when he returned. He locked the door and pulled the shade. "If I could dig myself a hole any deeper, I could be buried standing up."

"What's happened?" Conner held a broom. With Burl and Alice not working for Ian anymore, someone had to sweep.

"I saw Alice."

"She was in here asking after you."

"Did you tell her where to find me?" He studied Conner's face.

"No. I tried to get her to stay and wait for you. She said she'd come back. I'll guess she's not coming back."

"Only if I were dead."

Conner leaned the broom against the counter and stood next to him. "What happened?"

"She caught Burl and me walking along the street together. I think she was madder than when her grandfather tried to force her to marry me. It was like flaming arrows shooting out from her beautiful blue eyes." He never wanted to see her that mad or to disappoint her so again.

Conner frowned. "I'm really sorry. If I had known she was going to head that direction, I'd have forced her to stay. Then she'd only be mad at me."

"It's not your fault. I knew when she said she didn't want Burl in the store that she really meant she didn't want him near me." Burl had known it, too, and they'd both gone against her wishes.

"I don't know why she can't look at all this logically and see you were trying to help. If it's any consolation, I think she should do as her grandfather asked and marry you."

It was nice to have Conner on his side, but the only person that really mattered was Alice. He hoped Arthur was right and she would "simmer down." She had more to simmer down from now. But she had come to his store looking for him. That was a small consolation now that he'd angered her further.

❧

Burl stomped up the stairs ahead of Alice.

"Burl, be considerate of the other people."

He stomped harder, went into their apartment, and slammed the door before she got there.

Her head pounded. She hadn't the patience to deal with him right now. Once they both calmed down, she would recant her hasty decision. She shouldn't have told Burl he couldn't see Mr. MacGregor. If Mr. MacGregor wanted to spend his time helping Burl, it would be good. She'd felt hurt and betrayed—again—and the words had flown from her mouth. Oscar had done more than stolen their farm; he'd stolen her trust in people—trust she might have had for Ian.

Alice went inside. Burl sat on his bed with his arms and legs folded. She would let him think about what he'd done for a bit first. She'd tell him after supper. She made a simple meal of fried eggs and potatoes.

Grandpa pushed his plate forward and rested his elbows on the table. "Out with it, you two. You're both in snits, and I want to get this over with."

Burl folded his arms across his chest. "I hate her."

"Burl, that's no way to talk about your sister," Grandpa scolded.

He had a right to his anger. She'd been unreasonable. "Tell Grandpa what you did today."

"I ran into Mr. MacGregor, and we was just talkin'."

"We *were* just talk*ing.*"

He narrowed his eyes. "We *was jus' talkin'.*"

She took a deep breath at his defiance. "They planned it behind my back. Mr. MacGregor had a whole stack of books."

"We wasn't doing nothin' wrong." Burl stood.

"Sit down, young man," Grandpa ordered.

"I like Mr. MacGregor better'n you." Burl jabbed a finger in the air toward her then bolted out the door.

She stood to go after him.

Grandpa put his hand on her arm. "Let him go. He'll simmer down and be back."

She stared at the closed door for a moment then rubbed her temple and nodded. "I'm going to lie down for a while before I clean up the dishes." She wetted a cloth with cool water for her forehead and closed herself in her room.

She'd made a mess of things. Everything had been going well when she worked for Ian. She'd been unfair to him and to Burl. She closed her eyes and laid the damp cloth over them. She hadn't needed any help from Ian to turn Burl away from her. She'd done it all by herself.

Lord, I'll make this right for Burl. Please don't let Mr. MacGregor hold my actions against Burl. Let him still be willing to instruct him. And. . .and. . .

There was something more in her heart to pray, but she couldn't get the words to form.

And if she were fortunate, Ian would forgive her as well.

fifteen

Alice woke with a start. The room was dark, and no light was coming from under her door, either. She felt the bed next to her but didn't find Miles there. She lit the candle on the floor next to her bed. Miles wasn't anywhere in the room, so she opened the door.

Grandpa sat at the table hunched over as though he were sleeping. The small nub of a candle that had been on the table had burned down to nothing and gone out. Cooled wax lay in a white pool on the rough wooden surface. She held her light high and could see Miles curled up on Grandpa and Burl's straw mattress, but no Burl. She searched the room. Burl wasn't anywhere.

"Grandpa," she whispered.

He didn't move.

She set her candle down and jostled his shoulder. "Grandpa."

He moaned and raised his head. "I must've drifted off."

"Burl's not here. What time is it?"

Grandpa took out his pocket watch. "After eight o'clock."

She rushed out into the hall to see if he was sitting there waiting for them to notice he hadn't returned. Empty. She ran down the stairs and out the front door. An icy rain fell on her face as she scanned the street. She gripped her arms against the bitter wind. February was turning out to be as cold as January—maybe colder. Burl wasn't anywhere in sight. The bite in the chilly air pushed her back inside.

She ran up to the apartment and swung on the old coat that Marjorie and Sally had given her. "He's not anywhere. I'm going to look for him."

"I'll go, too."

She put her hand on his shoulder. "Stay with Miles. I don't need you out in this getting sick again. You just got rid of that cough. I can move faster than you."

"I just feel so useless. I want to do something."

"Pray I find him quickly."

Grandpa folded his hand into a fist and rested his head on it. Already praying.

She put on her straw hat and tied her shawl over it and under her chin before heading out.

She wandered aimlessly through the streets calling Burl's name. Where could he be? She ended up near the school. Yes! He might go there. She searched the grounds and around the building calling. He wasn't there.

She stopped in the middle of the play yard. She didn't know where else to look. Where would he go? *Lord, where should I look? Help me find him.*

They had quarreled about Mr. MacGregor. Maybe he'd go to the store. She hurried there. The underground sidewalk was dark. She felt her way along the storefronts until she reached the pharmacy—at least she thought it was—but found the door locked. She knocked but heard nothing. Mr. Jackson had to be there. He lived in the back. *Please don't let him be out for the evening or staying on the ship with his friend Captain Carlyle.* She knocked harder. This store was the only place she could think to look. If she had to, she'd break the window to wake him. He had to be here.

Fred started barking and getting closer to the door. Then she could see light behind the shade over the door window. The shade rolled up, and Mr. Jackson stood in a shirt, pants, and suspenders. He held the light close to the door and squinted.

She leaned into the light. "Mr. Jackson, it's me, Alice."

His eyes widened, and he immediately unlocked the door. "Mrs. Dempsey?"

"Is Burl here?"

"No." He stepped aside. "Come in."

She stepped inside. "Are you sure?"

Fred jumped up on her leg. Mr. Jackson pushed the dog away with his foot. "You're the only visitor I've had since we locked up. Why do you think Burl would be here?"

"We quarreled, and he ran off. I thought he might come looking for Mr. MacGregor." She looked about for any sign of Burl or Ian.

"He didn't come here."

Her heart plummeted. "Where else would he go?"

"You don't think he'd consider setting sail?" Mr. Jackson said.

"He hates the water. He can't swim."

"But you two did have a fight."

"Oh, Burl." She covered her face with her hands. *Please, Burl, don't have set sail just to spite me. Lord, protect him wherever he is.*

"Do you think he'd go looking for Ian?" Mr. Jackson asked.

She removed her hands from her face. "He doesn't know where he lives."

"That we know of. If he's not there, Ian might have a few ideas of where to look. At the very least, he would be one more person looking."

There was a slim chance Burl knew where Ian lived, and if he did know, he would certainly go there. "Where does he live?"

"Let me get my coat and shoes, and I'll take you." Mr. Jackson ran to the back with Fred on his heels. He returned lickety-split with a hat on his head and shoving his cast arm into one sleeve of his coat. Fred tried to follow them out the door.

"You stay here, girl."

Fred whined and wagged her tail.

"No, Fred." Mr. Jackson handed Alice the lamp and closed the door.

She could see Fred through the door on her hind legs, hopping.

Mr. Jackson locked the door and took the light.

"It's raining up there." She wanted him to be prepared.

"I figured as much."

"You did?"

He smiled. "You're dripping wet."

She looked at her coat sleeve. She hadn't thought that she must look like a half-drowned cat. "Is Mr. MacGregor's house far?"

"About half a mile."

When they broke above ground, the rain had slowed to a drizzle. Mr. Jackson guided her across the street and over a block. The rain began to come down harder again and sting.

"Hail." Mr. Jackson took her arm and pulled her up the street and into a doorway overhang. "We'll wait it out here."

Pea-sized ice balls bounced on the ground. "We can't stop."

Mr. Jackson held her in place in the confined area, his body shielding her from hail blowing in. "I'm sure it'll only be a few minutes." Mr. Jackson had to yell to be heard over the downpour of hail.

Burl was out in this somewhere. *Please let Burl be safely at Ian's.* She refused to give in to the tears that wanted to flow. What if Burl was at Ian's and Ian kept him from her? Would he do that?

"Ian only wants to help you." Mr. Jackson's level voice close to her ear startled her. "He cares a lot for you."

"Not after today. I've made such a mess of things. He'll likely never speak to me again." She wished she could take it all back.

"Sure he will."

She hoped so, but right now all she wanted to do was find Burl safe. She was so tired of being strong for everyone. So tired of struggling. She just wanted to give up. She resisted the urge to collapse into Mr. Jackson's arms and cry.

❧

"Amen." Ian raised his head and looked up at the clock on

his mantel. After nine. He should head off to bed. He closed the Bible that was on his lap and put it on the table beside his chair.

He'd been unsettled all evening. Usually reading the Word and praying helped calm his nerves and give him focus, but not tonight. He kept seeing Alice's angry face and the hurt he'd caused her. And the fury with which Burl had verbally struck his sister. That had wounded her. Ian had pleaded with God to show him how to make it all up to her.

He understood Alice's reluctance to trust him after her husband had taken advantage of her naiveté. He'd been naive once, too. It was hard to trust again.

He turned out the light on the table, and Tiny flipped over and stood in one fluid motion. "No, boy. You sleep down here." But as he banked the fire in the stove then blew out one of the lights on his mantel, Tiny was nowhere. He'd silently lumbered upstairs. Ian wasn't sure why he even tried to keep the dog out of his room. At least he'd succeeded at keeping him off the bed. So far.

He took the other mantel light and headed upstairs to bed. Maybe if he were lying down, his thoughts would finally settle. There was nothing he could do tonight to make things right with Alice. Maybe the solution would come to him as he drifted off to sleep or in the morning after a good night's rest.

A noise outside stopped him halfway up the stairs. Footsteps? On his porch? At this hour? He turned to head back down when a knock sounded on his door. Tiny bounded past him and stood by the door with a wagging tail.

Conner and Alice stood on his porch, dripping wet.

He opened the door wide. "Come in."

"Where's Burl?" Alice demanded as she stepped over the threshold.

"I don't know."

"Isn't he here?" The strain of panic laced her voice.

"No."

Alice frantically looked around.

He turned to Conner. "What's going on?"

"Burl ran away."

Alice grabbed his arm. "Please, if he's here, tell me."

"He's not. I wish he were." The anguish on her face made him feel like someone had just gutted him. "Come stand by the fire." He guided her over to the warmth.

"He has to be here. Where else would he go? I don't know where else to look." She stared into the fire for a moment then turned. "I have to go back out. He could be hurt."

"In a minute. You need to warm up a bit." He took off her wet shawl and hat then her soaking coat. He went to the kitchen and got two towels, handing one to Conner and the other to Alice. "Let me go dress, and I'll go looking with you. You warm up, and I'll be right back." He shot Conner a look that he hoped told him not to let her go anywhere. Conner gave him a nod, and Ian took the stairs two at a time.

He returned relieved to see Alice still by the fire. He waved Conner over. "Go back to the store in case Burl decides to show up there."

"I'm going to run by the docks first in case he decided to set sail after all." Conner handed him back the towel and put on his hat before slipping out the door.

Ian hoped Conner's cast would hold up in all the wet weather it was exposed to tonight. Conner would likely need a new one put on tomorrow.

Ian grabbed his two wool coats and wrapped the thicker one around Alice. "This ought to keep you warm." He wrapped the red scarf she'd made around her neck and tucked the end through the slit, pulling it snug.

"Why are you doing this?"

"To keep you warm. Your coat is all wet." He buttoned the coat.

She shook her head. "Why are you being nice to me and helping me?"

He smiled at her and set a sturdy old leather hat on her head. "I want to."

She began to cry.

He gripped her shoulders. "Don't cry. We'll find him."

"I don't know where else to look."

If Burl hadn't come to his house and he hadn't gone to the store, where would he go? "I have an idea." He took her hand and pulled her out the door with Tiny at their heels.

She stopped short on his porch. "It's snowing." She started crying again. "He must be so cold and scared."

It rarely snowed in the city. Why did it have to tonight? They crunched through the snow-covered hail. He headed in the direction of his store but stopped a few streets away at an empty lot.

Alice looked around. "What are we doing here?"

"This is where Burl and I 'accidentally' met earlier today. And the day before."

He heard her crying again. Sobbing actually. "Don't cry. We'll find him."

"It's not me crying this time."

He scanned the lot. "Burl?"

Tiny ran across the lot barking.

"Mr. MacGregor?" Burl crawled out from under a large, flat board covered in white that was leaning against the adjacent building.

Tiny put his paws on Burl's shoulders, pushing him back against the building.

"Tiny!" Ian called.

The dog licked the boy's face then sat down.

Ian held tight to Alice's arm to keep her from slipping as they made their way across the uneven snowy ground to the shivering boy with tear-stained cheeks.

Burl grabbed him tightly around the waist. "I prayed God would send you to me."

Ian took off his coat and wrapped it around the boy.

Alice took off the scarf, secured it around Burl's neck, and put her hat on his head. "You had me scared to death." Tears rolled down her face.

Burl wiped at his face with the too-long coat sleeves, which were wet and did little good. "I'm sorry. I thought I could find Mr. MacGregor's house."

Ian took Burl's arm and Alice's to steady them on the snow- and hail-covered ground. "Come on. Let's get you two where it's warm." Tiny bounded in front of them.

They quickly made their way back to Ian's house. He built a fire in the fireplace and stoked the fire in the kitchen stove and the potbelly stove. He was going to have his house as warm as he could get it.

He pulled two wingback chairs up to the fireplace. Alice had already taken the coat, scarf, and hat off Burl.

"Sit. Both of you." He went to the kitchen and poured what hot water there was from the teakettle into the pan he rinsed dishes in, then added cold water until the temperature was right. He refilled the kettle, put it back on to heat, and added more wood to the fire. He brought out the pan. "Take off your boots, and let's get those feet warmed up."

Burl shook. "I'm too cold to."

He began removing one boot while Alice untied the other.

Once the boy's feet were bare, Ian put them in the lukewarm water. He then pointed to Alice. "You, too."

"I'm fine." She shivered as she said it.

"Take them off, and I'll find something else to put water in."

He rushed through his house and brought back a ceramic washbasin and three blankets. "He needs to get out of those wet clothes. Can you do that while I check on the water?"

She nodded.

The water had barely begun to change temperature. He ran upstairs and brought back a quilt, a shirt, and a pair of pants. They would have to do. He handed them to Alice. "Here, put these on. You can change in the study." He pointed to the room off the living room.

"I'll be fine."

"You are soaking wet." He gripped her by the shoulders and pulled her to her feet, then guided her to the room and closed the door, leaving her with the change of clothes. He hoped she obeyed. He didn't want her getting deathly ill.

He took the towel from earlier and dried Burl's hair. "Are you warming up?"

Burl nodded.

"I'll make you some tea as soon as the kettle heats." He took Burl's wet clothes into the kitchen and hung them by the stove. The water wasn't hot yet, but he got out three cups and his plain white teapot. He put some more water in his largest pan and pushed more wood into the stove.

As he went back out into the living room, Alice came out of the study with the quilt wrapped around her, holding out her wet clothes.

He took them. "Thank you. Please sit and get warm."

"What about you?"

"I didn't get that wet. It was only snowing by the time I went out. I'll make some tea in a few minutes." He went back into the kitchen. All he could think about was getting the two of them warm. The large bottom pan was steaming, as was the kettle. He poured hot water into the teapot then some into the ceramic basin, mixing it until it was just warm, not too hot. He took the basin and the teakettle out to the living room. He put the basin in front of Alice on the floor and poured a little hot water into the pan with Burl's feet.

He left to retrieve the tea, and when he returned, Alice had her feet in the basin. He gave a mental sigh of relief. The unsettled feeling he'd had since that afternoon finally drifted away.

&

Burl lay curled up on the floor in front of the fire with Tiny for a pillow.

Alice stood and felt her drying skirt. "We need to get back home. Grandpa will be worried."

Ian went to the window. "It's still snowing a little."

"I can't stay knowing he'll be waiting up for us."

"Wait here. I'll be right back." He wished he'd put a phone in his home now but went next door and called a taxi. "There's a taxi on the way."

Alice stood over Burl. "I hate to wake him up."

"Then don't. I'll take you home now and bring him home in the morning. He shouldn't be out in the cold so soon anyway."

"I'll go change back into my clothes."

She scooped up her clothes and closed herself in his study. The clothes couldn't be dry yet, but she had to put them back on. She and Ian knew that nothing inappropriate had happened between them, but wearing men's clothing still wouldn't look good.

She returned in her yellow dress. "Where's my coat?"

"It's still wet. Take this one." He handed her the one he'd let her wear. "I'll bring yours in the morning with Burl."

She looked exhausted. She shouldn't be going out in this weather, either, but there was little other choice.

He peeked out the window as the taxi drove up. "It's here."

She gazed down at Burl and fingered his hair. "What if he wakes up before you get back?"

"He'll be fine. Tiny's with him. I'm sure he'll still be fast asleep when I return." He guided her outside and helped her into the taxi, then climbed in. "You mind if I make a quick stop at the store to let Conner know we found him?"

"That'd be fine."

He instructed the driver where to go and ran his errand as fast as possible. When he returned, Alice's head was tipped back. He slipped in next to her. She rolled her head onto his shoulder without waking. He smiled. Maybe after this she would reconsider him or at least consider coming back to work for him. It might be sly of him, but he was considering using tonight as leverage, to make her feel in his debt. She wouldn't like that, but he was desperate to keep her near him. He took a deep breath. It didn't sit right to use this circumstance against her. He would let it lie and see what the Lord brought.

When they arrived at her building, he was reluctant to disturb her. "Alice, we're here."

She mewed like a kitten and raised her head. "Did I fall asleep?"

"It's been a very long day for you." He jumped down then helped her down.

She looked up at him with a faint smile. "Thank you, Ian."

His heart thumped harder. He wanted to pull her into his arms and kiss her. In her present state, he thought she just might let him. Instead he turned her toward the door. "Wait here for me, driver."

He walked her up to her apartment. When he opened the door for her, Arthur said, "Amen," and immediately raised his head from where he sat at the table, a stub of a candle burned next to him.

Arthur stood. "Where's Burl?"

"He's asleep at my house. We thought it best not to wake him. He's fine though." Ian helped Alice off with her coat and hung it on the back of a chair.

Arthur held on to one of the chairs. "So he found his way to your house?"

"No. We found him in an empty lot, cold and wet."

Arthur turned to Alice. "You go on off to bed. I'll keep Miles out here with me."

Alice shuffled off to her room and closed the door.

He watched her the whole way, aching to help her, then turned back to Arthur. "I'll bring Burl by in the morning."

"Alice will sleep late. Why don't you take him to the store and bring him by after work?"

"I don't want to upset Alice any more than she already is."

"She'll be fine. She's simmered down." Arthur gave him a big hug. "Thank you."

"You're welcome, sir."

"Now you'll marry my granddaughter." Arthur cocked his mouth up in a wide smile.

The old man never gave up. Ian knew where Alice got her stubborn streak. "I'm not making you any more promises. I'm going to wait and see how Alice feels."

"She needs a man to help her. I don't know how much longer I'll be around."

He shook his head. "I won't force her. She'll only hate me for it."

"I'll be the one forcing her. She'll hate me."

"But if I go along with it, I'm just as guilty. No, Arthur, I won't agree to it."

Arthur dipped his head down and shook it. "Too bad."

"See what became of your meddling last time. Let it rest, Arthur." Though the old man didn't argue anymore, Ian wasn't one bit convinced Arthur would comply.

sixteen

Alice took a deep breath before entering Ian's pharmacy the next day. She wasn't sure what to say to him. Ian stood behind the counter, assisting a customer. He looked up at her and nodded, then motioned to Burl at the end of the counter. Was that it? Did he just want her to collect her brother and leave?

When she approached, Burl looked up from the book he was reading. His eyes widened, but he didn't say anything.

She combed his shaggy blond hair off his forehead with her fingers. He needed a haircut. "Are you feeling all right? You were out in the cold for some time yesterday."

He ducked out from under her hand and shook his hair back in place. "Don't do that." He glanced toward Ian. "I'm fine."

She sighed mentally. He was growing up. "What are you reading?"

"It's a whole book about Australia. It's a country and a continent. They have all kinds of strange animals. Look, this is a kangaroo."

She looked at the animal standing upright with short front legs and a long, thick tail. She'd never seen anything like it.

"It has a pocket in the front to carry the baby kangaroo called a joey, and it hops around, and it can balance on its tail and kick you with its back feet, and some people have 'em as pets, and they just hop around the house." Burl looked back down at the book. "I don't wanna leave."

"I think it's best. We don't want to impose on Mr. MacGregor."

"But I want him to teach me. I learn a lot more here than

152

at school, interestin' stuff."

Her heart went out to her brother. Maybe she could make small steps back into Ian's life. "We'll talk about this later."

"I don't mind." Ian spoke behind her. "I enjoy having the boy here. He's no bother."

She turned to him. "Maybe we should talk about this in private."

"Please, Alice," Burl pleaded. "I promise I won't be no trouble."

Ian nodded.

There was no point in talking in private now. "One of the reasons I came was to ask if you wouldn't mind instructing him again, but I didn't want to put you on the spot like this."

Ian put his hand on his chest. "Honestly, I would be proud to teach such an eager lad with a hungry mind for knowledge."

She smiled. "Thank you."

"Yee haw!" Burl danced off his stool.

"But I do have one stipulation." Ian gazed directly at her.

"What is it?"

"You come back to work for me."

She wanted the job but not out of charity. She wanted to be needed, really needed. "Mr. MacGregor, you and I both know that you hardly need me here. We both know I wasn't doing so well learning the medicines."

Ian shrugged. "That's my deal."

Burl grabbed her arm. "Pleeease."

She was sure that, even if she turned down his job offer, he'd still instruct Burl. "It seems I'm outnumbered, but if you don't have meaningful work for me here, I'll look elsewhere."

He held out his hand. "Deal."

She shook it. "Deal."

Ian continued to hold on to her hand. "Now you said that was one of the reasons you came. What is the other?"

"Um." She found it hard to think with her hand wrapped

in the warmth of his, so she pulled it away. "I wanted to thank you for helping me find Burl last night. Please, come to supper tonight." She wanted to begin to mend the bridge between them. Her heart needed to mend the bridge.

"Finding Burl safe is all the thanks I need. Besides, Burl has thanked me a number of times. You have already had me over for Sunday dinner. It's my turn to reciprocate. Please come to my house for supper."

"Grandpa asked you before, and, as I said, I want to thank you."

"I insist you come to my house. I'll send a taxi for you and your family around six."

She sensed if she protested any further, this would turn into another crate incident. "Very well, but next time I host."

He seemed pleased. Was it because she'd agreed to dine at his house? Or was it that there would be a next time? She found she was looking forward to both.

Ian put a hand on Burl's shoulder. "Can Burl go home with me and help with supper?"

Burl looked up at her, nodding.

"Very well."

Ian smiled at her, and warmth spiraled inside her.

⁂

Ian hustled around his house. He'd left work early and purchased a pot roast on his way home.

Burl came through the kitchen door from outside with an armload of wood. "You got a weepin' willow out back."

"Yes, I *have* a weeping willow tree. Your sister is going to reconsider my tutoring you if you don't learn to use better grammar."

Burl dumped the wood into the wood box. "I'm tryin'."

"Do you like willow trees?"

"Sure do, but they is—I mean they are Alice's favorite. She always says how much she misses the weepin' willow we had on our farm before Oscar died."

Her deceased husband. Maybe he could garner a little more information on the man. "Did you like your sister's husband?"

Burl shrugged. "He was all right, I guess."

"What do you mean by that?"

"He was around a bunch before they got hitched but only played with Alice. After they was married, he wasn't there so much. He had a lot of business in town."

So Oscar pretty much ignored Burl. "Do you know how to set a table?"

Burl wrinkled up his nose and shrugged.

"Start by putting enough plates on the table, one for each person. They're in the hutch in the dining room."

As Burl ran off into the next room, Ian looked out the window to the tree in the moonlight. It was good to know she would like his tree, but would she like his house? Then he went out to help Burl with the table.

"I like your house." Burl set the first plate onto the table. "I wish I lived here."

He wished it, too. Wait a minute. He looked about and took in the rest of the house. Why couldn't Alice and her family live there? He had plenty of room. If he moved his books and desk to the small room off the kitchen, Arthur could have the study for his bedroom. Miles and Burl could have one of the spare rooms upstairs, and Alice could have the other. No. That would put Alice across the hall from him. That would not be appropriate. He could move his study upstairs. No, then that would leave the little room off the kitchen for Alice. He'd take the room off the kitchen and move his desk and books to the smallest room upstairs, Burl and Miles could have the front bedroom upstairs, and Alice the biggest room up there.

He smiled to himself. That would work. He could definitely see Alice and her family in this house. But would Alice agree? He sighed. Only in his dreams. Maybe if he talked Arthur into it first and got Burl on his side, she'd have no choice.

He shook his head. She'd just think he was scheming behind her back again, because he was. But he was sure she was meant to be here in this house. He went to the mantel to retrieve the candlesticks. He frowned at the dust. He wished he had a housekeeper. He didn't want Alice to see his house like this.

Wait a minute. Maybe he did. If his house needed attention and if he intentionally burned supper, she would see he indeed needed a housekeeper, and he could ask her to be his housekeeper. No, he couldn't intentionally ruin perfectly good food, but she had been right when she said he didn't have enough work for all three of them at the store. His business was still good, but so many other businesses in the underground portion of the city were not doing so well. It was only a matter of time before the business underground waned. He should start looking for a store above ground. Maybe even build in that vacant lot.

Once Alice had agreed to become his housekeeper, he would tell her that part of her compensation was room and board for her and her family. That just might work.

"What you smilin' for?"

He turned to Burl. "Just making a few plans."

"I got the plates on the table."

He showed Burl where to find the silverware and instructed him where the pieces went on the table. He would wait until it was obvious there was not enough work for her at the store before he sprang the housekeeper position on her with her family moving in with him.

➤

Alice gazed around Ian's lovely home. It made her miss the farmhouse. Space to move around without tripping over someone and a room of her own. A garden out back to tend to and reap fresh vegetables from. Vegetables she could can and feed her family on all winter.

She fingered a doily on the small end table by the couch. Her ma had taught her to crochet doilies, but none so fancy as this. Had his ma made this one? Or a sister? Or fiancée? She knew so little about him.

"I'm sorry about the dust." Ian came up beside her. "I haven't had time to clean."

She looked closer. So there was dust. "This is beautiful work."

"My grandmother knitted that."

He obviously didn't know the difference between knitting and crocheting, but that didn't matter. "Supper was delicious. The pot roast was tender but not dried out. That's not easy to do. Everything was quite tasty. You're a good cook."

Ian's mouth turned up slightly at her compliment. "I've had to learn. I don't normally have time to cook so elaborate a meal. I usually eat more simply during the week. I often stay at the store and eat with Conner."

"You should have invited him."

"I did. He was tired. It was nice having a full table."

She nodded. "You have a very nice home."

"It's just a house. It takes more than one person to make a place a home, but tonight it has felt more like a home." The intensity of his gaze wrapped around her.

She felt warmth and love from him. Fear sprang up inside her. "We should be going. Thank you again for supper." But she really didn't want to leave. Part of her wanted to leave, to run, and another part wanted to say in his protection.

"I told the taxi to return at eight. We have a little time. I want to show you something." He helped her into her coat and led her through the kitchen and out the back door.

The snow had melted away in the day's rain, but the clouds had passed, and the moon shone brightly on a huge weeping willow tree bare of its leaves.

"Burl said you had a willow on your farm."

She smiled at the familiar shape of the tree and droop of the long, whiplike branches. "I used to love to climb it as a girl."

"You are welcome to climb mine anytime you like."

She put her hands on her hips. "In a dress? I climbed my last tree years ago."

He smiled at her. "My garden is over there." He pointed to a dirt patch on the side of the backyard.

"That's a large garden for one person."

"I share with neighbors and Conner." He stood next to her.

Her heart pounded against her chest at his nearness. "The taxi will be here soon. I should get Miles and Burl ready to go." They went inside.

"Can I stay here with Mr. MacGregor again tonight?" Burl turned pleading blue eyes on her.

"I'll not have you wearing out Mr. MacGregor's kind generosity. Now get your coat."

"I don't mind if he stays one more night."

Burl pressed his hands together. "Please."

"Let the boy stay." Grandpa shrugged his coat around his shoulders.

She was outnumbered again. "Since Mr. MacGregor said it was all right, then I'll consent."

Burl danced in a circle.

"Me, too," Miles said.

"No. You're going home with me." She picked up Miles and turned to Grandpa. "Are you coming? Or are you going to stay here as well?"

"Don't get smart with me, lass," Grandpa said in Gaelic.

"Thank you again for supper." She went out and climbed into the waiting taxi with Miles.

Grandpa said good-bye and climbed in. Once the carriage was in motion, he said, "You could do a lot worse than a man like Ian MacGregor."

"Grandpa, don't start with that." She was not getting married to Ian or anyone else, so there was no point in pursuing the conversation. But if she ever did, she'd choose someone like Ian, dependable and settled in his life.

She'd made up her mind when Oscar died that she would never again let a man deceive her, but all men weren't like Oscar. Maybe she'd made a hasty decision.

Thankfully, Grandpa remained quiet the rest of the trip.

seventeen

Two days later at closing time, Ian waited with Burl while Alice changed out of her work clothes to go home. "Burl, do you know what has your sister on edge today?"

The boy twisted the corner of his suit coat around his finger. "I'm not s'pose to say nothin' about it."

He pulled his eyebrows together. "Your grandfather isn't ill, is he?"

"Nope," Burl mumbled then looked up sharply. "But I don't understand him makin' her do somethin' she don't want to do. It's not right."

"I've learned that your sister doesn't do what she doesn't want to do. She'll be fine." He'd wondered why the boy was quieter than usual. Burl had had something on his mind.

"Makes me do stuff I don't want to do, either."

Well, he was still a boy and needed training.

Burl looked up at Ian sideways. "No one said I couldn't say nothin' about not comin' back to work here."

His gut twisted. "What? Alice is leaving?" Not after he'd just gotten her back.

"Me, too." Burl looked like his best friend just died.

Alice came out then from the back room.

He studied her delicate face and gazed deep into the pools of her blue eyes. "Is it true?" He could see that it was.

"Is what true?"

He didn't want to but had to voice it. "That you're quitting?"

She glared at Burl.

Burl shrugged. "No one said I couldn't say nothin' about that."

Alice composed herself and turned back to him. "I was

160

going to give you my notice before I left today."

Why would she leave now? He would talk her out of it. "Have you found another position?" And what else was there that the boy wasn't supposed to tell him? Something worse?

Tears filled her eyes. She shook her head. "Burl, go change your clothes. We need to be leaving."

"But Alice."

"Do as I say." The words were strained, and a tear slipped free.

"Come." Ian guided her to the back and sat her in a chair. "What's going on, Alice?" He caressed away the moisture on each cheek with his thumbs.

She bit her bottom lip. "Grandpa insists that I marry. He has found a businessman who needs a wife. I don't see how I can stop him this time."

He felt as though he'd just been punched in the gut. He couldn't draw in air. He couldn't lose her now. They were getting on so well. "What if you had a different job? And a better place to live?"

She shook her head. "He insists that I marry. He thinks only a man—a husband—can take care of me, Miles, and Burl when he's gone. He keeps reminding me that his time is short on this earth. I'm afraid if I cross him, it'll be too much for his heart. I don't want to lose him."

Ian could understand the old man wanting the peace of mind that his loved ones left behind would be all right after he was gone, but there were other means. "He will force you into this; you are sure of that?"

She nodded, and tears swam in her eyes.

Why did Arthur have to be so stubborn? Why did Alice? He knelt in front of her. "Then marry me. If you have to marry someone you don't want to, at least marry someone who loves you." Was that hope he saw in her eyes?

"You would do that for me?"

"Of course. I'd reach up and pluck a star from the heavens

if it would make you happy."

"It wouldn't be fair to you."

"God never promised us fair, but I know down to the depths of my soul that I am to take care of you and your family in whatever way you'll let me." He gazed at her a moment. "We can put the wedding off for a while." He would do just about anything to keep her and take care of her.

"But why? I've been so awful to you."

"No, you haven't. You were scared and struggling to provide for your family. I don't want to lose you."

"I thought I was in love with Oscar, but I know now that wasn't really love. I don't know what love looks like. I don't know if I'm capable of love."

There wasn't a thread of truth in that. "You love Burl, and Miles, and your grandfather." Her love was genuine and true. A self-sacrificing love.

"That's a different kind of love."

He took her hand in his. "Please marry me."

"Please, Alice, please." Burl stood behind him. "Then I can still get good learning."

He could tell where Burl's interest lay. He didn't care as long as it helped sway Alice to accept his offer. If she married someone else, he wouldn't be able to take it. He'd leave town.

She rocked her head back and forth. "All I can think is how it wouldn't be fair to you. You deserve someone who will love you back. Why would you want to marry me?"

He could give her a thousand reasons, but none of them formed into words. "I can't help whom my heart fell in love with."

"If I walk away, you can find someone who is capable of loving you."

"You are capable of loving. I would still love you. I would rather live the rest of my life with the woman I love—you— than live with a woman I don't love. My heart will always belong to you. Is it possible that you could ever love me back?"

Tears filled her eyes again. "I wish I knew. I don't know what love between a man and a woman is supposed to be like. Gran died before I was born, and Pa died just before Burl was born. My own marriage was lies, deception, and betrayal."

She wanted to love. He could see it in her eyes. She was afraid to try. "Are you willing to marry me and find out?"

She gulped a deep breath and nodded.

He smiled. "I believe with all my heart, which is bursting with love for you, that you will come to love me in time, in your own way."

"I wish I had your confidence."

"Yee haw! We're gonna be married." Burl jumped up and down. "I have to tell Mr. Jackson. And Fred and Tiny."

Both Ian and Alice chuckled at that. He took out his handkerchief and wiped away the rest of her tears. "As I said, you can decide how long you want to wait before the wedding, but I want you and your family to move into my house. I can turn the study into a room for Arthur, and you and the boys can take the upstairs rooms. There is a room off the kitchen I can use or I can stay here with Conner. Put a cot in the other storage room. But I want to do it soon. Tomorrow if possible."

Her gaze darted around his face. "Very well." She looked down at her clasped hands. "What about the businessman Grandpa made arrangements with?"

"I'll talk to Arthur. I know he'll agree to my marrying you." He pulled her to her feet. "One more thing. Since we are to be wed"—his mouth went suddenly dry; he tried to swallow—"may I kiss you?"

She gifted him with a gentle smile. "I'd like that."

Her lips were soft, and though he wanted to linger, he didn't. A light blush tinted her cheeks.

Later that evening at Alice's apartment, Ian sat at the table with Arthur while Alice washed up the dishes. "I appreciate your agreeing to a marriage between Alice and myself."

Arthur held out his hand, and Ian shook it. "I'll be proud to call you grandson." His grip was still strong.

Arthur's blessing was only half of it. "About the other man. Will that be a problem? I can talk to him if you need me to."

Arthur dipped his head and studied his cup of now cold tea. "Don't worry about that."

Ian got a strange feeling. He lowered his voice. "Arthur, there was another businessman you promised Alice to, wasn't there?"

"Other? There is a businessman." Arthur jabbed a finger toward him. "You. I just didn't tell Alice."

Scheming again. "You made her think we had an agreement?"

"Not really *we*. I just let her think I made arrangements with an unnamed businessman."

"But you and I had no agreement."

"You said you wouldn't force her. She just needed a little prodding to see what was good for her. I've prayed about this, and if I wasn't sure down to the depths of my soul that this was the right thing, I wouldn't do it. My granddaughter needs you, and you want her. I need to know she'll be well taken care of after I'm gone. Miles and Burl need a father. I know you'll take good care of my family."

"What happens when she finds out what we've done?"

"She needn't find out. And if she does, you two will already be married."

"Arthur, you're going to get me in trouble again. What if she finds out before we're married and calls it off?"

"She needs a husband."

He doubted Alice felt that way.

"If not you, I *will* find someone else." Arthur patted his hand. "Don't worry so much. You've done nothing wrong. Your offer was in good faith."

But he knew now. How would Alice take that? More

scheming behind her back. This was not good.

Arthur patted his hand. "She loves you."

Wishful thinking of an old man. "She told me herself that she didn't, but I'm hopeful she will one day."

"She thinks that because Oscar didn't really love her, she can't love. She just doesn't recognize that what's in her heart is love. She's afraid to acknowledge her love for fear of getting hurt again."

Ian hoped it was that simple, but he wasn't going to count on it yet. Once they were married, he would relax a little and give her the time she needed to fall in love with him.

❧

The next day at the store before opening, Ian leaned on the counter. "Should I tell her what Arthur has done?"

Conner put a bottle back onto the shelf. "I always vote for the truth. Secrets never gain you in the end."

"What if she calls off the wedding?"

"What if she doesn't?"

"Then everything is fine. But what if she does?" He couldn't lose her again.

"Then you won't be starting a marriage with a secret between the two of you."

Alice and Burl walked in then. He needed more time to figure this out.

Conner waved to them. "I hear congratulations are in order."

A smile pulled at Alice's mouth and spread up to her eyes. "Thank you." She looked happy, truly happy, for the first time since he'd met her.

Ian came around the corner of the counter to her. "May I speak with you privately?"

She nodded and headed toward the back. "What is it? Have you changed your mind?" She unpinned her hat, concern etched in her features.

"No, but you might." He paused. "Last night when you were cleaning up the dishes, Arthur told me something." He was dreading this confession, but it was better to have it out in the open than harbor it until it became a real problem, a secret. "I'm the other businessman he told you he was going to marry you to. I promise you that I didn't know. I was genuinely concerned he was going to make you marry someone else."

She furrowed her brow. "So there was no other man?"

He shook his head. "But I believe if you dissolve our arrangement, he *will* find someone else for you to marry." He wanted to quell her anger before it flared.

She was quiet a moment. "I do, too."

"We can wait as long as you want."

She thought a minute. "Is there any point in postponing the inevitable?"

He knew there wasn't. "I'm not going to pressure you into anything."

"Grandpa is." She squared her shoulders. "We might as well make the plans straightaway if you're willing."

He smiled. "Very willing."

Her smile came back.

❧

Two days later, Alice folded the old quilts she had made and ones her mother had made, and bundled the few other possessions her family still owned. Ian and Mr. Jackson would arrive soon to move her family. Ian had rearranged his house to accommodate them and had moved himself to a hotel until the wedding.

The crate caught her gaze, and she smiled; then she looked at her finger where the sliver wounds had healed. Ian had taken such pains to see that she was taken care of. He'd always tried to take care of her. From the first time she met him and he'd offered her a towel to dry off her face after coming down out of the rain, to getting her family out of this dirty little apartment. She looked back at the crate. It was silly, but she wanted to take it with her. They were leaving her bed and Grandpa and Burl's mattress and the table and chairs. None of the few pieces of furniture were going with her. She didn't need them at Ian's, and she didn't mind leaving any of it behind. . .except the crate.

"I know what you're thinking."

She sucked in a quick breath at Grandpa's nearness. She hadn't heard him come up behind her. How could he guess she had developed a sentimental attachment to a stupid crate? She turned to him.

Grandpa shook his head. "It's not fair to him."

Well at least she was sure he hadn't guessed about the crate. "What's not fair to whom?"

"Ian. You're thinking that once inside his house, you can put off marrying him, and he's so besotted with you, he'd let you." Grandpa frowned.

She smiled. "Thursday morning at ten. Ian spoke with his minister and ours. That was the soonest we could be married." She'd been so busy with all the arrangements that she'd evidently overlooked telling Grandpa that one important detail. "I planned for us to stay here until the wedding, but Ian wouldn't hear of it. He insists that we move now. I'm not sure if it's to get us out of this place or because he's afraid I might change my mind."

Grandpa smiled then. "Probably both."

The door opened, and Ian, Mr. Jackson, and Finn followed Burl inside. Burl looked around. "Is everythin' ready to go? We have a carriage waitin'." He was certainly eager to get out of this place.

"Everything is packed there by the door." Except the crate.

Burl grabbed up an armful of quilts and bedding and headed back out the door.

Mr. Jackson and Finn filled their arms and left as well.

"Are you ready to go?" Ian started gathering up the smaller bundles.

She nodded and grabbed the crate. "Let's put those in here."

She set it beside him and put in her knitting bag, the soup kettle, and frying pan. That should be easier to carry."

He smiled at her. "I'm marrying a practical woman." He hoisted the crate and went out.

A smile pulled at her mouth. She was getting to keep the crate.

Grandpa left with Miles. She took one last look around before crossing the threshold. Relief washed over her as she closed the apartment door for the last time. She'd be a married woman again soon. Strangely, that thought sat well with her.

eighteen

Alice stood, in a new white dress that Ian had bought her, at the back of her small church with Grandpa. She hoped she was doing the right thing, not only for herself but for Burl and Miles and Grandpa, as well. And for Ian. He deserved better than a half-willing wife. But she found that she didn't dread marriage as she thought she would. She was surprised to find that she was looking forward to being Ian's wife.

Burl and Miles sat in the front pew with Conner and Finn. Only a handful of people from her church could make it on such short notice, as well as a handful from Ian's church. The sum total of her family was here, but none of Ian's. His family lived too far away but would make the trip out in late spring. She'd offered to hold off the wedding until then, but Ian wouldn't hear of it. He said his family understood and wished them well.

As she started forward on Grandpa's arm, she looked up to the front where Ian stood in his new black suit. He smiled at her, and her breath caught. She stopped. It couldn't be. Her heart hammered hard against her ribs.

Grandpa held fast to her arm. "What is it, child?"

"I love him." The words came out in a whisper.

Grandpa chuckled. "I know, lass."

She turned to him. "How? I only just discovered it."

"I figured you were too scared to see the love right in front of you. That's why I insisted on you marrying him. I knew you'd eventually figure out you loved him back. Now there's a man up front concerned you have changed your mind."

She looked at her husband-to-be. He did look worried. His smile was gone, and his brow creased.

"I have to tell him."

Grandpa patted her arm with his stump. "You'll tell him later."

She made her way to the front with her revelation bubbling up inside her. She could see it now. The feeling that churned inside her every time she was around Ian was love. It had been there for so long battling for control and confusing her, but how it was free. She couldn't take her eyes off him. Grandpa gave her away and went to sit with Finn and the others. Ian said his vows; then it was her turn.

"Wait." It wasn't right to marry him like this. "I need to tell you something."

"It can wait until later." The V between Ian's eyebrows deepened, begging her not to change her mind.

"No, it can't. Then it'll be too late."

Ian closed his eyes. "Don't do this. Please."

She put her hand on his arm, and he opened his eyes. "Standing at the back of the church, I realized something. I know what love looks like."

He raised his eyebrows in question.

"You. I love you. I had to let you know first. I'm marrying you because I love you."

Ian's mouth broke into a wide grin, and he stepped forward as if to hold her but thought better of it in public and stepped back, turning to the minister. "You can go on now. She's ready to take her vows."

And she was. She couldn't wait to become Mrs. Ian MacGregor. She was going to enjoy being his wife.

Minister Pepper announced to Ian that he could kiss his bride.

Finally.

He kissed her tenderly and lovingly. She didn't want him to let go, but he had to. The ceremony wasn't over.

Minister Pepper smiled then presented them as Mr. and Mrs. Ian MacGregor. Then everyone gathered in the other room to congratulate the happy couple and share the simple wedding cake Alice had made.

That evening after all the festivities had died down, Alice's family settled in for the night. Grandpa had gone to bed in his new bedroom before she'd even put Miles to bed an hour ago.

She met Burl and Tiny at the bottom of the stairs. "You all washed up for bed?"

He nodded. "Alice? Are you happy here?"

A smile pulled at her mouth. "Yes. Are you?"

He nodded even harder.

Her whole family seemed happy here. "Off to bed with you now. And don't wake Miles."

Burl tiptoed all the way up the stairs with Tiny on his heels. The huge Great Dane almost looked as though he were tiptoeing, too. She turned and went to join Ian in the kitchen but stopped short in the doorway. Ian had one foot inside the crate they had fought over. Her crate. Their crate.

Ian grabbed one of the side boards and yanked it free with a *crack*.

She gasped.

He turned to her.

"What are you doing?" She took a step forward.

"I was just getting rid of this old crate." He pointed the thin board toward the open burner with orange glowing embers inside.

She hurried over. "You can't."

"Why not?"

She wanted to snatch the board from him. How did she explain what the silly old crate meant to her? Tears sprang to her eyes, and everything blurred. She tried to blink them away but only succeeded in pushing one out of each eye.

Ian set the board down on the covered side of the stove. "Don't cry." He caressed away her tears with gentle strokes of his thumbs. "We can keep it. I just thought it was a sad reminder of your life before."

She sniffled and successfully blinked back the rest of her tears. "You held my hand for the first time because of that crate."

He took her hand between his. "This one."

She nodded. "I think that's when I started falling in love with you, but it scared me, and I pushed the feelings away."

He released her hand, and picking up the board, he bent down and fitted the nails back into their holes and pushed the board in place. "Good as new."

She put her hands around his neck. "Thank you."

He put his hands on her waist. "I'd do anything for you." He pulled her close and kissed her.

"I love you, Mr. MacGregor," she whispered when he pulled away.

"I love you, too, Mrs. MacGregor." He smiled and kissed her again. Then he scooped her up into his arms and carried her upstairs to their bedroom.

A Letter To Our Readers

Dear Reader:

In order that we might better contribute to your reading enjoyment, we would appreciate your taking a few minutes to respond to the following questions. We welcome your comments and read each form and letter we receive. When completed, please return to the following:

Fiction Editor
Heartsong Presents
PO Box 719
Uhrichsville, Ohio 44683

1. Did you enjoy reading *Uncertain Alliance* by Mary Davis?
   ❏ Very much! I would like to see more books by this author!
   ❏ Moderately. I would have enjoyed it more if

   _____
   _____
   _____

2. Are you a member of **Heartsong Presents**? ❏ Yes ❏ No
   If no, where did you purchase this book? _____
   _____

3. How would you rate, on a scale from 1 (poor) to 5 (superior), the cover design? _____

4. On a scale from 1 (poor) to 10 (superior), please rate the following elements.

   ____ Heroine   ____ Plot
   ____ Hero   ____ Inspirational theme
   ____ Setting   ____ Secondary characters

5. These characters were special because? _____
_____
_____

6. How has this book inspired your life? _____
_____
_____

7. What settings would you like to see covered in future
Heartsong Presents books? _____
_____
_____

8. What are some inspirational themes you would like to see
treated in future books? _____
_____
_____

9. Would you be interested in reading other **Heartsong
Presents** titles? ❑ Yes ❑ No

10. Please check your age range:
   ❑ Under 18   ❑ 18-24
   ❑ 25-34   ❑ 35-45
   ❑ 46-55   ❑ Over 55

Name _____
Occupation _____
Address _____
City, State, Zip_____

WYOMING
Brides

3 stories in 1

In the wilds of old Wyoming, three women face insurmountable dangers. Can they trust the Lord to preserve their love through the trails of life in the wilderness?

Historical, paperback, 368 pages, 5³/₁₆" x 8"

HEARTSONG
PRESENTS

If you love Christian romance…

$10.⁹⁹

You'll love Heartsong Presents' inspiring and faith-filled romances by today's very best Christian authors…Wanda E. Brunstetter, Mary Connealy, Susan Page Davis, Cathy Marie Hake, and Joyce Livingston, to mention a few!

When you join Heartsong Presents, you'll enjoy four brand-new, mass market, 176-page books—two contemporary and two historical—that will build you up in your faith when you discover God's role in every relationship you read about!

Mass Market 176 Pages

Imagine…four new romances every four weeks—with men and women like you who long to meet the one God has chosen as the love of their lives…all for the low price of $10.99 postpaid.

To join, simply visit www.heartsong presents.com or complete the coupon below and mail it to the address provided.

✁ -

YES! Sign me up for Heartso♥ng!

NEW MEMBERSHIPS WILL BE SHIPPED IMMEDIATELY! Send no money now. We'll bill you only $10.99 postpaid with your first shipment of four books. Or for faster action, call 1-740-922-7280.

NAME_____

ADDRESS_____

CITY_____ STATE _____ ZIP _____

MAIL TO: HEARTSONG PRESENTS, P.O. Box 721, Uhrichsville, Ohio 44683
or sign up at **WWW.HEARTSONGPRESENTS.COM**